WHITE WARRIOR

Center Point
Large Print

Also by Lewis B. Patten and available from
Center Point Large Print:

Lawless Town
Shadow of the Gun
Cañon Creek
Gun This Man Down
Giant on Horseback
Hang Him High
The Cheyenne Pool
Lone Rider
The Tired Gun
Five Rode West

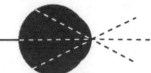

**This Large Print Book carries the
Seal of Approval of N.A.V.H.**

WHITE WARRIOR

Lewis B. Patten

CENTER POINT LARGE PRINT
THORNDIKE, MAINE

*To Cliff and Lewis, my sons,
who I hope may some day find
pleasure in reading this book.*

I. THE BOY

Chapter One

IT SEEMS AS THOUGH, if a man sits down with the conscious determination to go back over his life, he can remember a great deal of it, even back to when he was a boy. His mind is likely to skip around quite a lot, and he forgets many things, but the things he does recall are likely to be the most important that have happened to him.

Of it all, I suppose, the thing that sticks most in my mind is the slaughter at Sand Creek, for every detail of that day is etched in my memory as though it happened only yesterday.

I remember my friends, the bloody remnants of the six lodges of Arapaho who had been with Black Kettle's band of Cheyenne, and the way we burrowed in a cut bank like badgers at nightfall, huddling close together so we could get what warmth there was out of each other's bodies. Moccasins were worn through on those that had them, and bloody feet left a trail in the deep, crusted snow. Now and again there would be a body to mark the side of the trail where we'd passed by.

They call Indians savages, but I doubt that I'll ever see more savagery among the Indians than I saw practiced that day by Chivington's ninety-day volunteers. Nor will I forget the half a thousand dead, among them almost all the women and children, lying where they fell, mutilated beyond belief and bearing mute witness to the so-called civilization of the huge Methodist preacher and his men.

How anyone escaped, I'll never know. But a few of us did. And once out of sight, we didn't worry too much about leaving sign, for we knew there were many trails leading away from the village on Sand Creek. Chivington's bunch couldn't follow them all. Probably they were too busy mopping up survivors and mutilating the dead to follow any. Besides, we knew that the volunteers were anxious to disband. Their term of enlistment had almost expired. So it wasn't likely they'd go chasing across the snowy plain after a handful of beaten survivors.

I had no real place among the Arapaho any more, having left them once. But I'd helped them all I could when I'd seen how things were back there, and I'd stayed with them afterward, considerably mixed up in my mind as to which I was going to be, Indian or white.

Until the day I die, I think, I'll be able to see Left Hand's strong, calm face as we crouched that first night under the cut bank, waiting for morning and unable to sleep, talking out the torment that was in us both by the eerie, cold moonlight that sifted down through the thin layer of clouds overhead.

It was Left Hand that convinced me I should write this story down. He thought perhaps it would help the cause of understanding between Indian and white.

I'm not sure whether it will or not. Perhaps too much blood has already been shed. Perhaps there is too much hatred on both sides. But Indian or white, Left Hand is the wisest man I've ever known. And besides, I gave him my word.

I was nine when Ma and Pa left Independence for Santa Fe. Pa had always been a trader, and every year he made a trip up the Missouri with the keelboats to trade. It was a hard life, but then, Pa was a hard man. I can remember him saying time and again that there wasn't anything a goddamn Frenchy could do that he couldn't.

But trade on the upper Missouri kept falling off a little more each year because of increasing competition and the smallpox plague, which nearly killed off some of the tribes. At last, early in 1846, Ma talked Pa into outfitting a caravan for Santa Fe. Her family scrounged around and got together part of the money, and Pa somehow managed to borrow the rest.

There had always been trouble between Ma

9

and Pa that I'd never quite understood. But I do remember one particular time when I came up on them unexpectedly and found them quarreling. They were both furious, and saying things that I know they didn't really mean. Pa glared at me as though I were to blame for everything and told me to get the hell out. Among other things, he called me a "goddamn little bastard," a term I remember because I had to ask one of the older boys I played with what it meant.

Maybe Pa thought I wasn't his, and who's to know whether he was right or not? He was gone eight or nine months out of the year. But I remember my mother fairly well, and I have an idea Pa was wrong about her.

Pa was a hard-eyed, still-faced man with long, light hair and skin like a piece of old rawhide. His shoulders were broad and powerful, and his neck was thick and corded with muscle.

He never petted me or praised me for some little thing I'd done. He seemed to hate me, although I never hated him. A boy's got to have something to look up to, and I looked up to Pa because he was what I wanted to be when I grew up. An adventurer. An Indian fighter.

There were a few rare times, however, when he'd seem to forget for a while what it was about me he didn't like. Then he'd yarn aloud and I'd sit there spellbound, listening, looking up at his face and thinking that some day I was going to be just like him.

It seemed to me that preparations for the caravan lasted forever, but at last we were ready, with a dozen high-wheeled wagons loaded with trade goods and well covered with canvas to keep out dust and water.

We had forty men, or thereabouts, most of whom had a share in the venture, and a herd of spare riding horses and mules, as well as a bunch of spare oxen. There were several reasons Pa used oxen, one of which was that the Indians have no use for them and rarely bother to steal them.

Leaving was a wonderful adventure for a boy of nine. I imagined myself already grown, and could hardly wait until we reached Indian country. But it wasn't long before the journey lost its sheen of newness and became only monotonous. I began to spend the afternoons riding in the old, dusty carriage Ma traveled in, toward the head of the column. Usually I'd catch myself a nap, lulled to sleep by the rocking motion of the carriage on its springs.

From Independence we traveled west to the Arkansas River, and along that to the Caches and the Cimarron crossing of the Arkansas. There we loaded water into every keg we had and set out across the Jornada del Muerte, where the bones of those that had tried before lay bleaching beside the trail, where their wagons stood tilted and half buried in the sand, whitened until they looked like bones themselves.

Tempers were edgy by the time we reached the Cimarron River. Pa stopped there for a few days to soak wagon wheels, grease axles, and fix the things that needed repairs.

Most of the men got rested up, and their tempers improved. But not Pa's. He knew that now we were heading into Comanche and Kiowa country, and would be fair bait for both those tribes and the far-traveling Cheyenne and Arapaho. Nor was he sure that we'd be all right when we got to Santa Fe. There'd been rumors, even back in Missouri, of war with Mexico. Pa figured the Mexican governor, Armijo, might decide to confiscate everything the caravans brought in.

The morning we started on again, I caught up my old short-legged mule as always, and rode to the head of the train to get out of the dust. Behind me, the caravan unwound from our three-day camp site like a sluggish snake.

The sky seemed to stretch away for a million miles, blue as a robin's egg and without a cloud in it. Beneath it was the land, its belly-high grass dry and brown, with fresh green grass coming on underneath. A new country, different from anything I had known before. And exciting, because somewhere out across its endless distance were villages of hide tepees, and teeming thousands of bronzed, painted, befeathered savages.

Pa's harsh voice cut in on my thoughts as he rode up behind me. "Goddamn it, gimme that mule an' git your ass into the rig with your ma. This here's Injun country, an' they don't give a damn what they eat, boy meat or buffler meat."

All the good went out of the day for me. I slid down off the mule, dropping the last few inches because my legs were short. I looked around, expecting a howling, painted savage to materialize from behind each clump of grass. There were goose bumps on my arms.

I stood there, alone and small in the immensity of country around me, waiting with nervous fright for Ma to come up with the rig. There was a Mexican driving it, I remember, and as soon as he pulled up, I climbed in.

Ma gave me an absent smile, her eyes on Pa's broad back, retreating down the column. If I'd been noticing, I'd probably have seen the old hurt in her eyes, the loneliness, and perhaps a certain desperate quality that asked, "Will he never change?"

She was a pretty woman, and not heavy-set like most women back home. She had big brown eyes like those of a deer, but she never really seemed to see me. She took care of me and saw I had what I needed, but that was all. Her mind was always on Pa, and troubled because of the way he was with her, and puzzling about how she could change it.

This morning she seemed uneasy. She sat up straight, and after Pa went out of sight she stared across the treeless land as though she were actually afraid of it. I guess she was putting a lot of hope in this venture, and praying that when they arrived, opened their store, and were together all the time, maybe Pa would change in his feelings toward her. But the Lord had other plans, because neither Ma nor Pa ever got to Santa Fe.

We hadn't gone over two or three miles from where we'd camped when we came to a long, steep hill. The caravan started up, mounted guard first, then our carriage, after that the wagons. Back at the very rear came the oxen, and off a little to one side the herd of horses and mules, grazing as they traveled.

The grade was too steep for the oxen. So, just as they'd done a dozen times before, men dropped back from the guard in front, and others came up from the rear. They dismounted and let their horses stray out to one side of the caravan to crop grass while they helped the wagons along by grabbing wheel spokes and straining hard to move them forward.

It must have taken the better part of an hour to reach the top. The guards' horses had strayed out pretty far from the trail, but I didn't pay much attention until I saw the war party that came howling down on us from the tall bluffs to our right.

I'd have said there were at least a hundred of them, but probably there weren't more than thirty at most. Likely they'd been waiting since sunup, knowing from watching other caravans exactly what would happen when we hit the grade.

Half the party rode at a wide gallop down the flank of the train, gathering up the guards' horses and mules as they went, and driving them before them. When they reached the rear of the caravan, there were a few shots and away the Indians went, with our whole herd of horses and mules.

Meanwhile, the rest of the war party had been galloping back and forth along the flank of the train, firing their guns and screeching at the tops of their lungs. I was scared, but fascinated too, for this was what I'd been hoping to see ever since we'd left Missouri. It never occurred to me that before long I'd wish I'd never seen an Indian.

They'd have pulled off as soon as the rest of their party got away with the horses, and all we'd have been out would have been the spare animals, but right then the team pulling the carriage, mules that only this morning had been roped green out of the herd, began to snort and buck, and before the driver could do much, they bolted away from the trail and out across the top of the hill.

This was more than the Indians had bargained for, but they didn't waste any time taking advantage of it. Screeching like madmen, they rode in behind us, cutting us off from the rest of the train.

The carriage was slamming around on its springs, nearly pitching both Ma and me out. She yanked me down, threw a buffalo robe over me, and then flung her own body down on top of me.

I thought I'd suffocate under that robe. I wriggled around until I could get my nose out in the air. I was facing the rear of the carriage, and suddenly I saw Pa coming, riding his big bay mule and galloping through the blinding cloud of dust toward us. His face, in the brief glimpse I got of it, was different than I'd ever seen it before. All the still-faced, sour bad temper was gone. Its color was almost gray, and his lips had no color at all. But I saw his lips move, as though he were shouting my mother's name, Lisa. Then the dust cloud obscured him.

The corner of my eye caught movement, that of an Indian riding at full tilt up beside our mules. He shot three or four arrows at either the mules or the driver.

What happened afterward isn't too clear. I remember total blackness as Ma pushed my head back under the buffalo robe. Then the world was spinning around crazily, and there was an awful crash as the carriage went over on its side. My head must have struck something mighty hard, because I lost consciousness. I came to hearing Ma's shrill screaming.

Everything that had happened came back to me with a rush, the Indians and the crash of the carriage. But I was still in darkness, muffled up under the heavy robe. As much afraid of its smothering confinement as of the Indians, I clawed my way out.

Ma's screams had faded, as though they were farther away now. But something was in the carriage with me, and it couldn't be anything but an Indian.

No use saying I wasn't scared. Even now, thinking of that day has the power to start chills along my spine. But I kept telling myself that I'd wanted to be a man like Pa and that now was the time to start. In the back of my mind, of course, was the memory of Pa riding toward us, and of the forty men with the caravan, who were surely on their way to help us.

The Indian was down on his knees, pawing around, looking for something to take, I suppose. He had Ma's tortoise-shell comb stuck in his greasy hair, and for some reason that helped. Fury mixed with the fear in me, and made the fear fade.

I jumped on his naked back, biting and clawing and kicking as hard and fast as I could. He swung around, grabbing me, his face all twisted, but when he saw I was only pan-sized, he began to grin. I fought all the harder, remembering what Pa had said about Indians' eating boy meat, but he held my back against him with an arm like iron and climbed out of the carriage.

As he dropped to the ground, I got my chance and squirmed around and sank my teeth into the naked flesh of his belly.

He let out a howl and dropped me. I scrambled up and began to run. Another Indian, younger than the first, let out a yell and grabbed my hair with one hand while the other hand snatched a tomahawk from his belt. But the first Indian grabbed the younger one and said something in Indian talk to him. The young one let me go, although it was plain he didn't want to.

Almost immediately after that, all the Indians jumped on their horses and lit out, because the men from the caravan were coming on afoot, firing as they came. The Indians that had me rode out in one direction and the three or four that had Ma rode out in another, with her still struggling and screaming my name.

Off and on all day, I struggled and fought to get loose. The Indian that carried me only laughed and held on tighter. But there's a limit to the terror a person can stand. After a while, exhausted from fighting, I quieted and went to sleep.

That night the Indian gave me some dry, hard meat that tasted as though it had berries in it.

Pemmican. When I was finished, he tied my hands and feet with leather strips.

It was completely dark after the fire died out, but I didn't go to sleep. I lay there hearing the Indians snoring, hearing the horses fidgeting around and cropping grass nearby. I wondered if I'd be rescued in time, before the Indians decided to eat me.

My face twisted up and tears burned behind my eyes. When it got so bad I couldn't stand it any more, I buried my face in the blanket the Indian had covered me with and bawled like a baby.

It helped, and I felt better when it was done. Later the young Indians who had carried Ma away came into camp, but Ma wasn't with them now. All the rest of the Indians laughed and called to the young ones, but of course I didn't know what they said.

I told myself that Pa had rescued her, and that he'd be coming for me soon. I made myself believe it, too. In fact, it was several years before I'd face up to the certainty that both Ma and Pa were dead, even though I saw scalps the next day among the war party that looked like their hair. I suppose there are times when a person's mind closes in on itself so it won't have to think about something it doesn't want to face.

Among the horses and mules the Indians had stolen from the train was my own short-legged mule, and the next day the Indian who had caught me, Red Stone, put me on my mule and let me ride along beside him. A couple of times, feeling the mule under me and thinking perhaps I could get away, I tried it, but both times Red Stone overtook me and brought me back.

He didn't seem angered either time. He only grinned and chuckled, and looked at me as though he were proud I'd tried to get away. But he took no chances. Every night he tied my hands and feet with those strips of leather, which made it hard to sleep.

Perhaps a boy is better able to understand someone of a strange race than an adult. Gradually, as we traveled, I came to the conclusion that Pa had been wrong, that these Indians had no intention of eating me. It just didn't seem reasonable that they'd be kind to me if that's what they were planning.

And Red Stone was kind. Riding along, he'd try to teach me to talk Arapaho. He'd point to himself and say, *"Neisa-na,"* until I'd repeat it after him. Then he'd point to me and say, *"Nei-ba,"* and I'd say that too.

At first I thought Neisa-na was his name, and Nei-ba the name he'd given me, but later I found out the words meant "father" and "son." He'd adopted me to take the place of his own son, who had died the winter before. Otherwise, I'd have been as dead as Pa and Ma were.

Once we saw a deer and Red Stone pointed,

saying, *"Bihii. Bihii."* So I knew the word for deer. And by the time we reached the village on the Purgatoire, I knew several more words and could recognize them when they were spoken.

A mile or so short of the village, the party halted. Laughing and talking, in high good spirits, they fired a patch of grass. After the flames had been stamped out, they took the black soot from the ground and rubbed it on their faces, chest, and arms. Except for the way they were laughing, paying no attention to me, I'd have got scared all over again.

Talking in a soothing monotone, Red Stone carefully smeared some of the black on my own face, and that seemed to please the whole party.

We rode in then, driving the stolen animals ahead. Pretty soon we passed another Indian who was standing all by himself on the top of a little knoll. His face was covered with some kind of grayish-white paint, and he wore a white buffalo robe. In his hand he carried a white club decorated with feathers.

Red Stone pointed to him and said, *"Ga-ahine-na,"* which I later learned meant "coyote-man." He was one of the camp scouts that kept constant lookout for enemy tribesmen from promontories near the village. This one looked to be middle-aged, and he yelled as he waved us on.

The village had perhaps thirty tepees in it,

arranged in an irregular circle and all facing east. Dogs began to bark as we drew near. Men and women and children came running out. When they saw the black soot on our faces, they began to yell and laugh and dance up and down. They clustered around the men of the war party. They poked and pinched me until I kicked one of them, and then Red Stone said something sharply and they let me alone.

Red Stone hustled me into a tepee that was almost as big as our whole parlor back home. An Indian woman brought me some food and clucked over me while I ate. Everything was so strange and frightening that I wanted to cry, but I managed to control myself and not do it.

Homesick and all alone, I sat there looking at them, suddenly hating them, until they got up uneasily and went away.

Chapter Two

RED STONE and his squaw seemed to know I wouldn't run away in the daylight, or else they knew I'd not be able to get far, with all the other Indians around. But at night, for almost a week, they tied my hands and feet as though I were an animal they wanted to tame and couldn't trust to stay.

Most white people believe that an Indian is stoic and impassive, but they don't understand Indians very well, or they'd know better. Probably the only Indians they've ever seen have been those at powwows with the whites, where the Indians always try to act solemn, and where they're suspicious and cautious, as they surely have reason to be.

Indians are people like anyone else when they're not on guard. They laugh and joke and act like fools sometimes. The women cry when they're hurt, and so do the children. What an Indian feels is mighty plain in his face if a person takes the trouble to look.

Red Stone's squaw was called Beaver Woman. All day long, that first week, she clucked over me like a mother hen, smiling, trying to make me smile too. At least a dozen times a day she'd feel my arms and legs, which were thin, and then go get me food out of the iron pot simmering over a tiny fire in the center of the lodge. She'd bring it to me in a bowl hollowed out of a cottonwood knot, or sometimes on a rawhide plate, and she'd give me a horn spoon to eat with.

Every time she'd feel my arms and bring me food, I'd think of what Pa had said. Then I'd look at Beaver Woman's face and know it wasn't true.

Naturally, being full, I couldn't eat every time she tried to feed me. So to tempt me she hunted up delicacies like the roots of cattails, which tasted very much like the little new potatoes we had in the early summer back home. She cooked meadow larks, and once a puppy Red Stone had killed specially for me. The puppy tasted a whole lot like veal. She made me hot, fragrant tea from the dried leaves of a wild peppermint plant, and sometimes gravy from bone marrow mixed with dried chokecherries.

Red Stone brought me a small bow and a handful of arrows, which pleased me a great deal, as it would any boy, white or red. He combed and braided my hair, though it was shorter than that of the Indian boys, making a braid to lie on each side of my head the way the Arapaho wore it.

And Beaver Woman gave me clothes, a buckskin shirt, fringed and decorated with colored porcupine quills, and leggings to match. She gave me two pairs of moccasins that fitted perfectly, though she'd made no moccasins or anything else since I'd come. I learned later that when her own boy died she'd kept right on making clothes for him, as though somehow her mind wouldn't face the fact that he was dead.

After I convinced myself they weren't going to hurt me, there was one part of me that reveled in these new experiences and in the gifts they gave me. Yet all the time there was another part of me that was frightened, and homesick, and all alone.

The lodge was comfortable, too, except on still days, when it was filled with smoke. The floor was covered with buffalo robes, and there were floor-level chairs, really only seats and chair backs, made of willows bent and woven together.

That first week I remember crying a lot in the night when I didn't think anyone would hear. Nights were the times I really got homesick for Ma and Pa, and then I'd build dreams in my mind in which I'd find them after fighting my way across the miles that separated me from where I'd last seen them. In these dreams I was quite a hero, riding a stolen paint horse and lugging the scalps of all the Indians who'd tried to stop me. I'm quite sure I knew they were dead. I just wouldn't face it.

A couple of times, although I was very careful to make no sound, Beaver Woman came slipping silently to me in the night, felt my wet face with her hands, and then caught me up close and held me tight against her while she crooned soothingly to me in Arapaho.

After seven or eight days, the whole village packed up and moved. The tepees came down and were rolled up and lashed to travois poles. Everything else was packed the same way. Even the dogs dragged small travois packed with food and clothing and household things. By noon the village was moving north, raising a cloud of dust that could have been seen for twenty miles. Red Stone had over fifty horses, and it took twelve of them to move his lodge and the things in it. Off to the east traveled the horse herd, slow and easy, the animals grazing as they went.

Though I didn't know it then, the village moved because of me. They could have denied attacking Pa's caravan except for the fact that I was living proof they were guilty. And they'd got to wondering if there wouldn't be some retaliation from the Long Knives.

Again I rode my short-legged mule, staying close beside Red Stone. Traveling, he continued to teach me the Arapaho words for things, as well as the sign language common to all the plains tribes.

He'd changed me until I looked like just another Indian boy at a distance. But he couldn't change the color of my eyes, nor could he make me feel like an Indian just because he made me look like one.

The children of the band showed considerable curiosity about me. Several times I got separated from Red Stone, and each time the Indian children would cluster around me, jabbering among themselves and reaching out to pinch or poke me or pull my braids. They wanted to be friendly, but I didn't know that. So I made up my mind the next time it happened somebody was going to be damned surprised.

After that I tried to stay with Red Stone, but during the rather considerable confusion of making camp, I got separated again. Watching that confusion, you'd think everybody and every-thing had suddenly taken leave of their senses. You'd think order could never emerge from it. Horses squealed and pitched and kicked out at the men trying to unburden them. Dogs fought and yipped, or just sat and barked. The children screamed and cried and ran back and forth, and the squaws screeched at them, trying to make them behave.

Red Stone and Beaver Woman were familiar to me by now, and therefore comforting. They were comforting, too, because their eyes always had a pleading look, as though they hoped I would like them and want to stay with them of my own free will. So when I lost track of them, even for a short while, I'd get frightened and an empty feeling would come to my stomach.

It was the beginning of a feeling that has

troubled me all of my life at one time or another—a feeling of being alone, even in a big crowd of people; of being an outcast and not knowing what to do about it. I've never been able to forget that I'm not an Indian and therefore don't really belong with them. In later years I found out I didn't belong with the whites any more, either.

A man fights many battles during his lifetime, battles in which no blood is shed. They are battles with himself. Most men win and go on, leaving the battleground behind. But my battleground was never behind. It was always with me. Perhaps while there is hatred between Indian and white I can never leave it behind.

Camp was being pitched on the bank of a little creek among a big grove of cottonwoods. As soon as I missed Red Stone, I began to look around for him.

Eight or ten boys my age and older were out gathering buffalo chips and wood for fires. I began to do the same, working away from them and hoping they wouldn't notice me. They spotted me, though, and stopped what they were doing. They came over and made a circle around me. I didn't yet understand enough Arapaho to know what they said, for they talked rapidly and sometimes slurred their words together. But when they started to poke and pinch me, I began to get mad.

I suppose it's the same everywhere. Friendliness expresses itself in mock hostility. But I was carrying a good-sized chip on my shoulder because I didn't belong among them. I was hurt and angry, so I sailed into them.

There were too many, of course. But I fought with my fists the way boys did back home, and for a while I did pretty well. Then I found myself down at the bottom of a pile, my face ground into the dirt and my arm twisted until I thought it would break.

An Indian broke it up and scattered the boys with a few vigorous kicks, leaving me all by myself, bawling and madder than I had ever been before. The Indian looked at me with plain dislike, said the word for Red Stone, and pointed. I shuffled in that direction, forcing myself to stop bawling.

I'd gone only a little ways when I heard something behind me. I swung around, ready to fight again if need be, but it was only a little Indian girl, looking as frightened as a trapped cottontail, but standing stubbornly still for all her fear. She stared at me, then looked down at the ground and scuffed her worn white moccasins in the dirt. I turned around and went on, and heard her coming too.

It was humiliating to have her see me with the marks of tears on my face, and I was out of sorts anyway. The second time I swung around so fast she bumped into me before she could stop. I said nastily, "Git, goddamn it! You git!"

She didn't understand the words, but she must have understood the meaning of my scowling face and threatening manner.

She didn't move. I wanted to hit her, but because she obviously expected it, I couldn't. I turned away and this time she stayed where she was, although I knew she kept watching me even with my back turned, offering friendship and not caring that I was different from the Indians.

But I'd got myself into a frame of mind that wouldn't accept friendship, or even recognize it when it was offered. I'd made up my mind I would always be a stranger among the Indians, an outsider that didn't belong and never would. I decided right then that as soon as possible I'd escape and go back to the whites. I even remember telling myself that I didn't want to belong with the Indians or anywhere else. But I did want to—more than anything else.

The fight that night wasn't the last. It seemed as though, in the five or six weeks that followed, my life was one long succession of fights, until even Red Stone looked disgusted with me.

The old men of the band talked to him, pointing at me. Their faces were grave and worried. By this time I'd learned considerable of the Arapaho tongue, and could tell what they were saying. They were urging him to take me to a place called

Bent's Fort. They told him the Long Knives would pay a ransom for me.

But Red Stone only closed his face against them and shook his head.

Chapter Three

ONE NIGHT I heard Red Stone and his squaw talking about me inside the tepee, so instead of going in, I sat down outside and listened.

Beaver Woman was saying, "Will you take the boy to the fort of the Long Knives?"

There was a long silence. I could imagine Red Stone, sitting cross-legged on the floor, puffing slowly and thoughtfully on his stone pipe. I waited nervously for his answer, and at last he said, "No. It is my fault he is as he is. The boy is white, and different from us."

Red Stone used the Arapaho word for spider, *niatha*, which was what the Arapaho sometimes called the whites. To an Arapaho, the spider is an almost magical creature, able to spin webs of great strength from his body, able to set snares with the webs and thus catch his food. Therefore the Arapaho likened the white man, also a being of superior skill, to the spider.

Red Stone went on: "He feels he does not belong among the Arapaho. And that is my fault, because I have not taught him our ways. I have not made him want to belong."

There was another long silence. I could almost see Beaver Woman in my mind, her eyes downcast, her hands nervously busy with some task or other while she waited tensely for Red Stone's decision. She was a good wife, and would not question his decision, whatever it was.

My own mind was almost as tense as hers must have been. For some reason, the idea of going back frightened me, perhaps because I realized in the back of my mind that Pa and Ma were dead, and that going back would only be going to strangers.

But the decision was not mine. It was Red Stone's. He said at last, "I will take a journey with the boy. I will teach him the ways of the Arapaho, for only by knowing us can he become one of us."

No more was said. But next morning Red Stone caught up a couple of horses and we left the village, carrying nothing but our weapons and a blanket apiece. We headed toward the mountains in the west, toward the tall, barren, snow-covered peaks.

The sky was so blue it almost hurt the eyes to look at it, and white, puffy clouds drifted across it. Flocks of small birds, flushed from the grass as our horses traveled through it, circled us and alighted again. In the distance I saw a herd of buffalo, and, nearer, half a dozen antelope stared at us curiously.

Red Stone's face might have been called typically Arapaho. His nose was long and straight.

His eyes, wide-set above it, were large and at their outer corners crinkled with a thousand lines of good humor and laughter. His mouth was generous and firm, his chin strong without being formidable.

He talked slowly, calmly. "In the beginning," he said, "all the earth was covered with water, save for a single mountain. Upon this mountain sat an Arapaho, who was a god. He taught the people how to live, how to make pipes of stone and hollow reeds, how to make bows and arrows with which to kill game, how to make fire by rubbing two sticks together, how to tan the hides of the buffalo."

I thought about asking where the people were if all the world was covered with water, but I kept still, mostly because Red Stone was so solemn.

"The Arapaho lived north of the great river, but long ago they came south because there were buffalo and horses here."

I listened attentively, because there was something about Red Stone's manner that made me listen. He told me the customs of the Arapaho, their history, their religion. He told me who were their traditional enemies, the Pawnees, the Shoshones, the Utes, the Bannocks. He told me who were their friends, the Sioux, the Cheyenne, the Gros Ventres, the Northern Arapaho or Sagebrush Men.

I thought Red Stone's code of ethics rather

strange, perhaps because it was so different from a white man's. It was all right to steal from an enemy; in fact, it was downright honorable if you did. You could steal his horse, his women, you could even take his life.

With your friends it was different. You weren't supposed to fight with them or steal from them. If a man killed a friend or ally, or stole from him, he was an outcast from that time on.

The Indians' ethics seemed strange to me that day. I have since revised my opinion somewhat, realizing that they were in a continuous state of war with their enemies, and realizing as well that during wartime the white man's code becomes very similar to that of the Indian.

Time slipped past swiftly. We halted at noon, when Red Stone killed a rabbit with an arrow. He built a fire, showing me how it was done. Tonight, he told me, I could try it myself.

After we'd cooked the rabbit on sticks over the fire, we ate, and after that Red Stone taught me the right way to hold the bow, the way to release the arrows so that they flew straight and true.

He taught me the game called *chi-chita-ne*, in which you hold a small bundle of grass in your right hand, bow and arrow in your left. You toss the grass into the air, and are supposed to put an arrow into it before it can touch the ground.

I couldn't do it, of course, but Red Stone could,

easily. While I stubbornly kept trying, he smiled at me and patted my back.

"This is the way for a boy to belong to the Arapaho," he said. "Do not fight them. Understand them. Learn their ways, for they are good ways."

In the afternoon he showed me how to throw myself to one side of my horse's neck, clinging with a foot on his back, an arm across his neck.

For three days we traveled, and for three days Red Stone talked to me. His voice was always calm and quiet, his face always patient and kind. Some of the bitter torment faded out of me during those three days. No longer were the Arapaho strange to me, and therefore fearsome. No longer was I resentful and defiant.

On the third day we crossed a divide with the wind like a swift bird beating through the pines, and could look down upon the vast, mist-shaded Bayou Salade, hunting ground of our enemies the Utes.

Here, where danger lived with us constantly, we stayed. And here I began to think of myself as an Arapaho, son of Red Stone.

I could now make a fire by rubbing two sticks together. I could put an arrow through the bundle of grass before it touched the ground. And at last, one day, I killed my first game, a small brown cottontail.

Red Stone seemed inordinately pleased as I

carried it into camp. He told me that it was cause for great rejoicing among his people when a boy killed his first game. It showed that he would be a great warrior and a great hunter, a credit to his tribe and a good provider for his family.

That day we saw dust in the distance, dust that materialized into a hunting party of Utes. While they were not headed toward us, Red Stone decided it would be wise to depart, so we mounted our horses and set out for the home village.

Red Stone seemed satisfied with the progress I had made, and I'll admit I was quite proud of it myself. I'd grown to like this tall, muscular, kindly-faced Indian, to understand him. I made up my mind I'd make him glad he'd taken me for a son.

Down the valley of the Platte we rode, living off small game and wild berries, bathing each morning in the icy waters, sleeping each night under the countless stars, which were brighter here by far than they were down on the plain.

Those were the early days, the good days, before the whites dotted the plains and the banks of mountain streams with their shacks, before the Indian became poor and hungry and dirty. The land then was like a virgin woman, making a man feel that no one had trod its paths before.

The jay scolded us as we passed, the elk lumbered from our path, the deer stared at us with liquid, frightened eyes. Fish jumped in the tumbling white water, and the beaver smacked his tail against the still surface of his pond as we paused to drink. Pine was a pungent, pleasant smell that filled the air when the sun shone hot upon its boughs, and dew glistened upon the long grass in early morning.

But the mountains dropped behind and we came down upon the plain, and headed at last toward the village of Red Stone; toward the village I felt I was ready now to accept as my own.

It was nearly dusk when we raised the village smoke ahead of us in the still, warm air. Almost immediately, Red Stone halted, and sat his horse very quietly while he listened to the sounds coming from the village.

I didn't notice much difference, but Red Stone apparently did. A change came over his face. His expression became strange, wanting, almost hungry, and he seemed to have forgotten me altogether.

He kicked his horse into a run suddenly, and though I drummed on my own horse's ribs with my heels, I was unable to keep up with him.

Just short of the village, however, he seemed to remember me again. He halted, and as I pulled up he looked at me as though he could see right through me. His eyes had a glitter to them that had never been there before. A small chill ran down my spine.

"Go to the lodge and wait," he said in a strange voice.

I slid down off my horse and handed him the reins. He rode away, tugging my horse along behind.

Walking into the village, I noticed a difference about it myself. There weren't any men around, only squaws and children, and not too many of them. But outside the village, on the far side, was the noisiest, most caterwauling commotion I'd ever heard.

My first thought was that there was trouble, that some other tribe was attacking the village. But there wasn't any gunfire, nor did the noise sound like fighting.

I knew I ought to go to Red Stone's lodge, the way he'd told me to. But I was curious, and wanted to see what was going on. I slipped through the village toward all the noise, and stopped beside a tepee at its edge, watching.

The men out there were white men. I could tell that from their heavy beards, though they were dressed just like the Indians. They had a couple of wooden kegs unloaded on the ground, and a small pile of other things beside them. One of them was dipping into one of the kegs with a tin cup. He'd hand it to one of the Indians, and the Indian would drink and cough and gag. Then the white man would dip it in again and hand it to another Indian. Meanwhile, all the other men of our village were yelling and dancing and stamping around.

I knew what was in the keg, of course. It was whisky. What I didn't know was how it affected Indians, or what they'd do for it.

The men of the village who weren't yelling and dancing stood around the keg like a bunch of hungry dogs, but now suddenly the trader was shaking his head. His voice was harsh and hoarse, and he kept saying, over and over, "Trade, now. Trade for robes," first in English and then in Arapaho.

It was an old trick, not a nice one—gifts of enough whisky to make the braves wild for it, then refusal so they'd bring out the buffalo robes their squaws had made to trade for more.

The Indian men drifted away from the traders and came toward the village. I saw Red Stone coming, a little unsteadily, and ran for the tepee before he could see me.

I beat him inside by no more than half a minute. Beaver Woman looked at me steadily as I came in. She was sewing on a pair of moccasins with a bone awl and a piece of sinew. There was an odd wideness to her eyes, a strange sort of tension to her body.

She got up and started to get me something to eat out of the pot, but right at that moment Red Stone came in and Beaver Woman seemed to forget everything but him.

Red Stone paused just inside the entrance flap, swaying back and forth, peering at her as though he couldn't see very well. Beaver Woman backed away.

Red Stone went over to the far side of the lodge and picked up a pile of buffalo robes, maybe six or eight of them. They were beautiful things made of soft-tanned buffalo hide, decorated with fancy quillwork. Around their bottoms was a fringe made from the dew claws of buffalo, and on one there were dozens of tiny fawns' hoofs, so that a man wearing one would make a continuous rattling noise as he walked.

Beaver Woman blocked Red Stone's way as he headed toward the door. I'd never seen her face like this, scared, but stubborn too. She said in a low, frightened voice, "A wise man trades when the sun is in the sky—when his mind is clear—not when it is fogged with the medicine water."

Red Stone's face twisted the way it had done that day in the carriage when I'd jumped on his back. He flung out an arm to brush her aside. His forearm caught her full in the mouth, and she staggered across the tepee and fell. She lay there, blood trickling from a corner of her mouth, looking up at him. Her eyes were like those of a wounded deer. Red Stone went out, staggering under the weight of the buffalo robes and the liquor he'd consumed.

I could feel myself shaking all over, and I

didn't want to look at Beaver Woman. The quarrel between her and Red Stone reminded me of the quarrels Ma and Pa had had. I thought of the white traders out there, realizing for the first time that if I went to them they'd take me back.

But I knew I'd have to wait.

After a while, Beaver Woman came over to me with a bowl of meat. I didn't really want to eat, but she kept urging me, and once I got started, I realized how hungry I'd been.

While I ate, she talked, her fingers nervously busy again with the moccasin. "The white traders have come—three of them led by the one called Sonofabitch Smith."

Then she was silent. Outside the dogs were barking, and beyond the edge of the village a wolf was howling at the moon. Somewhere a squaw was sobbing, and over it all I could hear the shrill whoops of the Arapaho men out at the traders' camp.

As though she were talking to herself, Beaver Woman whispered, "They have brought much medicine water. It will turn our men to animals, and in the morning they will have the gagging sickness only to show for the robes they have taken to trade."

I knew that sonofabitch was a cussword, and asked, "Why do they call the trader Sonofabitch?"

"Because he speaks the word so often."

I finished eating and buried myself in my robes.

43

I didn't try to sleep, but I couldn't have slept anyway, what with all the screeching going on.

Gradually, though, it died away as one after another of the Indians slept from the effects of the strong drink. In the glow from the dying fire I studied the sleeping form of Beaver Woman. Then carefully I slipped from under my robes and sneaked out the door flap.

Cautiously and silently I went through the village toward the traders' camp. They had a big fire going, and by its light I could see them clearly, big, dirty men with eyes that were tiny and mean. Two of them were a little tipsy, but the third, whom I judged was Sonofabitch Smith, was cold sober, and kept looking toward the village with hot, hungry eyes.

Suddenly I was more afraid of the three than I was of the Indians. Without making my presence known, I crept back to my bed in Red Stone's lodge, where I snuggled down gratefully.

Outside the braves were still coming back. Some of them made it to their tepees, and some just fell down anywhere they happened to be. Red Stone came in and collapsed just inside the door flap. Beaver Woman got up and covered him, making me wonder if she had heard me leave a few moments before.

She freshened the fire and by its light pried the things Red Stone had in his hand from his tight-closed fingers. A scrap of red cloth. A mirror. A steel awl. That was all—that and the gagging sickness he'd have the next day.

Three of the braves in our village traded their squaws for their last drink of the medicine water. They brought the three traders into the village as the last sounds of the drunken orgy were dying away, and showed them into their lodges before they collapsed.

Lying there, I heard the squaws' protesting voices and the white men's obscenely cursing ones, and remembered the hot look in Sonofabitch Smith's eyes. After that, there was only silence. I lay utterly motionless, though every muscle in my body was as tight as a fiddle string. I wished I would go to sleep and not wake up.

After a long, long time, my eyes began to burn. My muscles relaxed, tears came, and I shook with silent sobbing. But at last I slept.

The next day there was much whipping of squaws and children in the village, and much sickness among the men. Down at the creek they sat, gagging and vomiting and holding their heads.

The white men were gone, and perhaps it was well they were gone. The braves of our village were angry now, and knew they had been cheated. The traders would not have been safe among them today.

But, as I later learned, an Indian's craving for whisky is strong, and his memory of being cheated is short after the sickness has worn away. Sonofabitch would come again, and others like him would come. I would watch the Arapaho traditions of decency and honor ground into the dirt under the influence of the medicine water, and would grow to hate the white men with a bitter intensity, as already some among the Indians did.

Chapter Four

ONE OF THESE among the Arapaho who hated the whites was an eleven-year-old boy named Two Antelopes. Always before he had been a ringleader whenever a group of Indian boys tormented me.

He was taller than I, and almost two years older. With the others, tormenting me or egging me into a fight had been a sort of game, but with Two Antelopes it had been deadly serious. Perhaps it was his way of striking back at the whites.

On the morning after the traders left, I went to the stream to bathe as I always did, only this morning I went farther upstream, in order to stay clear of the surly, touchy braves.

I found a spot and skinned out of my leggings, breechclout, and moccasins. I walked into the stream and squatted, splashing water up over me. Finished, I walked out, shaking the water from my body.

Above the waist, I was almost as brown as an Indian from going without a shirt. But below, where breechclout and leggings had been, I was startlingly white.

Standing there, drying in the sun, I was startled when a gob of black mud struck me on the flank.

I looked around, and there stood Two Antelopes, eyes narrowed, face all twisted up with hate. One of his eyes was black and nearly swelled shut. There were scabbed welts across his shoulders and chest from a whip. His lips were puffy and cut.

His voice was savage, and it lashed me like a curse. "Vulture! Flesh eater! I hate the whites! But mostly I hate you!"

Arapaho have no curses, no profanity. They find it hard to understand how white men can profane the God they profess to worship. But a worse insult cannot be offered than to call another a vulture, or to accuse him of eating flesh.

It wasn't hard to see that Two Antelopes was after a fight, and that he wouldn't be satisfied until he got it. He looked as though he'd already had one fight, but I knew he hadn't. His father had beaten him.

Two Antelopes' father was Eagle Feather, a stocky, short-statured brave who was supposed to be part Comanche. Eagle Feather was one of the warriors who had traded his squaw to one of the white men the night before, and Two Antelopes had no doubt been forced to lie there inside the dark tepee and listen while the trader took her.

Suddenly I wanted to apologize to Two Antelopes for my white blood, although I knew it wouldn't help. It would only brand me as a coward.

I also knew I was going to get licked. Because

no one can fight well when his heart isn't in it or when he understands too well the cause of his opponent's anger.

But I had to go through the motions. I spoke my half-hearted defiance in English unthinkingly: "I reckon you're a goddamn liar, Two Antelopes. I reckon you only hate the whites you figger you can whip." So wildly did his eyes flare at the sound of English that I switched into Arapaho. I was so mad myself by now that I didn't bother to explain what I'd already said in English. "You can stop hating me, because I'm one white you can't beat."

He began to grin eagerly as he came toward me, though his eyes weren't grinning. They were as hard as two pieces of stone, as cold as the eyes of the lynx.

Two Antelopes was dressed in breechclout, leggings, and moccasins, as I had been, which gave him a definite advantage. I was naked as the day I'd been born. The stones of the stream bank would bruise and cut my feet as we fought. The brush would scratch my naked body. But there was no time to dress.

He came at me slowly, as though he were waiting to see me break, and wanted to give me time to get good and scared. This tactic worked, too, but I was damned if I was going to let him know it was working. I began to move toward him.

It was then that he snatched the tomahawk out

of his belt, where I'd failed to noticed it before. It wasn't a play tomahawk, either. It was real, probably Eagle Feather's own.

I had been scared before. Now I was terrified. I wanted to run but knew I wouldn't. Even young as I was, even scared as I was, I knew that if I ran I'd be running all the rest of my life. Yet to stay and fight was to die. One blow of that tomahawk and I'd be finished.

My eyes darted back and forth, searching for something, some weapon with which I could fight back.

So intent were we both upon what we were doing that neither of us noticed the stealthy approach of a small party of Indians through the brush that lined the stream. One moment we were alone, and the next, four strange Indians stood there in a circle around us.

I didn't recognize them by tribe, but apparently Two Antelopes did, for his eyes widened with fright and he seemed to forget me. He turned to run, but his retreat was blocked by two of the grinning painted braves. Two Antelopes breathed the word for Pawnee.

One of the Pawnees grunted, and when I looked at him he tossed me a knife.

I caught it instinctively, luckily by the handle instead of by the blade. I stood there holding it, and the grinning Pawnee who had tossed it signed for me to go ahead and fight.

Nothing could have been farther from my thoughts. I hadn't wanted to fight Two Antelopes in the first place, and I wanted to even less now.

Nor did Two Antelopes feel any differently. He had no eyes for me, but kept glancing fearfully around, searching for a way to escape.

Then, as though we had both come to the same decision at once, we broke and ran. Two Antelopes darted between two Pawnee braves. I thought for a minute he'd get away, but one of the Pawnees stuck out a foot and tripped him. Two Antelopes sprawled face down in the mud.

They'd been watching him more closely than they had me. And by some freakish chance, I was the one that broke through.

I'll never know why I didn't just keep on running until I got to the village. I suppose my thoughts weren't working too straight. Anyway, instead of running, I circled and darted toward the spot where Two Antelopes had sprawled on the ground. I let out a yell that must have carried all the way to the village.

Of course, right away the Pawnees switched their attention from Two Antelopes to me. They knew they had to shut me up, and quick, before my yelling brought the whole village down on them.

Two of them converged on me, apparently forgetting the knife I still held in my hand. I slashed at an arm that reached out and the knife bit through flesh and scraped on bone. The Pawnee howled.

I darted past him, still heading toward Two Antelopes, who was up now and drawing the tomahawk back as though to throw it at me.

I ducked instinctively, but the tomahawk was not intended for me. Thrown with surprising skill, it struck the Pawnee brave just behind me full in the face.

Then the pair of us, myself and Two Antelopes, were racing together toward the village.

Two Antelopes raised his voice in a frantic cry, "Pawnees! Look out for the enemy!" and ahead of us the village came to life.

A brief rain of arrows fell around us. One of them pierced the calf of my leg and I fell as though I'd been tripped.

The pain was maddening, almost blinding. I lay on the ground, gasping and groaning, watching Two Antelopes going on and waiting for the Pawnees to come up and kill me. I rolled over onto my back, still clutching the knife.

But Two Antelopes wasn't leaving. As soon as he realized I was down, he stopped and came running back.

Had not the warriors in our village come so quickly, we would both have been killed. But even as I sat there waiting for the Pawnees to reach us, they halted. Then they were gone, fading into the brush like shadows, and past us came the men of our village, sick from the effects of the white men's medicine water, but also glad to have something on which they could vent their surly, smoldering anger.

Two Antelopes squatted beside me. He put a knee on my leg and yanked out the arrow in my calf.

All of a sudden everything grew blurred before my eyes. Red light flashed, and blinding white light, and everything began to spin around. The pain in my leg felt like a hot iron.

Two Antelopes was lifting me, and someone was helping him. I tried to see who it was, but things were too blurred.

We were heading back to the village, I supposed. Part of the time it seemed as if I were floating on a cloud. The other part of the time it was dark and silent. In one of my few clear-thinking moments I wondered if I were dying.

My ears were hearing other noises, too: the squawling of the squaws and children in the village, the whooping outside the village, the angry howling of our own men. Over it all I heard the high squealing of horses and the thunder of hoofs.

Even in my dazed state, I knew what that meant. The Pawnees were running off our horses. And upon the ability of our warriors to save enough horses to ride depended the life and future of our village.

Two Antelopes and the one helping me, the girl Waanibe, which means Singing Wind, managed to get me to Red Stone's tepee, and right away Beaver Woman took over, with Singing Wind helping her.

Beaver Woman gave me some mescal buttons to chew and made a poultice out of ground mescal buttons and placed it over the wound. Singing Wind squatted beside me, watching the pain in my face and crying softly.

I grinned at her and said with foolish bravado, "It ain't nothin'." She didn't understand, so I repeated it in Arapaho. I felt big and brave and strong. A feeling of importance was something I'd needed desperately, and because she gave it to me, I conceived an instant affection for her. Singing Wind was the same little girl who had followed me the night we'd pitched camp and I'd got lost from Red Stone.

She fingered her amulet, a small, beaded buckskin bag in the shape of a lizard in which a child's umbilical cord is preserved from birth, and kept watching me with her big, brimming eyes.

After a while Two Antelopes came forward fearfully. He said, "You will tell Red Stone what happened at the stream?"

I knew this was my chance to get even with Two Antelopes for his hatred and for his persecution. I don't know why I didn't say yes.

Maybe being the center of attention made me feel magnanimous.

I said, "It is already known what happened. I was bathing. As you came to the stream to bathe, the Pawnees jumped us. We fought and then ran. You stopped to help me when I was hurt. I will tell Red Stone that and no more."

Two Antelopes looked at me for a minute. Plainly he didn't believe me. Then he got up and went out of the lodge. A while after that, Beaver Woman chased Singing Wind out too and told me to sleep.

There is probably some drug in mescal buttons, because it was not long before the pain in my leg became less and I got drowsy. I went to sleep.

When I awoke, it was to a great noise within the village. Squaws were screeching, as they always did when the men came back from some foray or other. After a while the flap of the lodge lifted and Red Stone came in, followed by a young warrior I had never seen before. Their faces were smeared with soot, and in the stranger's belt was a dripping scalp. By this I knew at once that the horses had been recovered and the Pawnees defeated with no casualties to our men.

Red Stone looked at me with pride, but he spoke to the stranger. "This is my son, and today he has done well. Naked at the stream, he fought the Pawnees and drew much blood from one who tried to seize him. You are young, Left Hand, almost too young to be a warrior. Yet you have counted many coups already and will one day be a great chief. Will you do me the honor of naming my son?"

I supposed that Left Hand, of whom I had heard, had arrived at the village for a visit just in time to take part in the recovery of the stolen horses.

He spoke stiffly, acknowledging the honor of being asked to name me, pleased because it was the first time he had been so asked. He and Red Stone sat down, and Red Stone lighted his pipe with a twig from the fire. Then he pointed the pipestem at the heavens, at the earth, at the four points of the compass. He smoked a few moments and then passed the pipe to Left Hand.

Left Hand smoked and for a long time afterward they sat in silence. Left Hand kept looking over at me, and then at the ground. At last he said, "The boy is not of our tribe. He is *niatha*, is he not?"

Red Stone said, "He was taken in a raid on a white wagon train in Comanche country. I have adopted him to replace my own son, who died. The spirit of this one reminds me of the spirit of my own son."

This seemed to satisfy Left Hand, who got up and left the tepee. Red Stone went out with him, probably to start making arrangements for a feast to celebrate the naming ceremony. And I drifted back into an uneasy, painful sleep.

Left Hand stayed in our village with the two older warriors who accompanied him for a week. He stayed in our tepee, for Red Stone and the father of Left Hand had been chums during their boyhood. Having him stay with us was a great honor, for it was generally conceded among the Arapaho that Left Hand would one day be chief of all the Southern Arapaho, although he was now but eighteen years old.

For a young man, he was very thoughtful and solemn, not given to joking and skylarking, as were the young braves of our village. Already he seemed to possess the wisdom of one much older, and even Red Stone recognized this, for he asked Left Hand's thoughts and opinions on many subjects.

I remember clearly lying there in the lodge listening to Left Hand's measured, thoughtful tones as Red Stone asked him about the future of the tribe and what its relations with the whites should be.

Left Hand said, "Six seasons past, in the spring, I fasted for seven days on a mountaintop. I had neither food nor water, but only my pipe and a little tobacco. I was seeking knowledge of how to live, as is the custom among our people.

"For the first six days nothing happened. I

stared at the blazing sun, at the drifting white clouds in the sky. I shivered at night under my thin blanket. I thought I would freeze in a sudden spring snowstorm.

"And then, on the seventh day, Ha-sananen, Everybody's Father, appeared before me. But he was not an Arapaho. His skin was white and his eyes were blue. He had a beard, a great tawny beard like the waving grass in the midsummer."

Left Hand smoked thoughtfully for a long time. I was utterly silent, and Beaver Woman seemed to shrink down into her robe. Red Stone looked steadily at the ground immediately in front of him.

I was awed. I knew from what Red Stone had taught me that few men will relate their experiences during a fast, that it is part of their "medicine" and usually almost sacred. That Left Hand was now telling his medicine to Red Stone revealed his high respect for Red Stone and also his assurance that none of it would be repeated. Red Stone did not speak or ask questions, but only waited respectfully.

At last Left Hand said, "Ha-sananen spoke to me. 'There will be fighting and death. But the white men are as many as the buffalo, as many as the grains of sand in the river bed. Among them are good men and bad, as it is among the Arapaho. If your tribe is to live, it must learn to live at peace with the whites.' "

Red Stone and Beaver Woman stared at Left Hand as though he were a god himself, but Left Hand appeared not to notice them, or to be aware of his surroundings at all. He looked as if he were in a trance.

"He told me that the buffalo would disappear from the country of the Arapaho and Cheyenne. He said that the time would come when the Arapaho would become very poor. White men would pour over the plains like locusts, and would take from the Arapaho lands that have always been theirs. In return they would give the Arapaho much medicine water and worthless trinkets, and would lie with our squaws while we squatted before our tepees and offered no protest."

Red Stone said fiercely, "Never!"

"It is what Ha-sananen has told me."

Left Hand's chin sank down onto his chest and I thought he was asleep. Red Stone got up angrily and stalked from the tepee. After a few moments Left Hand followed.

The next day, the day of the naming, Red Stone went around the village, inviting the old men to the feast. Beaver Woman together with two or three other women of the village, spent the morning in preparing the feast.

When the time came, they all filed into the tepee. Left Hand, who was to name me, sat first at the left of the entrance. When they were all seated, Red Stone spoke to them. "This is the son who has come to live with us. Pray that he will grow up to be a good man, and a great warrior among our people. Pray that he will learn well the ways of the Arapaho, and that he will respect those ways."

He pushed me over to Left Hand, who touched me on the head and breathed into my face. Everyone was very solemn. Left Hand said, "I name you Sharp Knife, and pray that the old men of the pipe shall watch over you. I pray that your food shall be good and the water in the stream clear, so that you may grow up to be strong and brave."

He hugged me and patted me on the head. Then the old man next to him said, "Come here, Sharp Knife."

The name was strange in my ears, but it was mine, and this was the first time I had been called it. I went to him. As Left Hand had done, he hugged me and patted me and prayed that I would grow up to be strong and kind.

I was passed all the way around the circle. At last I reached the entrance, where Red Stone and Beaver Woman stood together. Red Stone led me out of the tepee and left me. He went back inside.

I sat down beside the pole tripod that held Red Stone's white buffalo-hide shield and his iron-tipped lance. I could hear them talking inside the lodge, and knew they were smoking. Before long now they would feast, and then the naming ceremony would be over.

I was proud of my new name, Sharp Knife, yet I'll admit I was somewhat disappointed that Left Hand hadn't named me after some warlike deed he'd done. Still, Sharp Knife was a good name, and was recognition of a deed of my own.

Best of all, the name seemed to make me an Indian myself, more than anything else could have done. I felt that at last I was going to belong, to be a part of the tribe. Yet I could also realize that it wouldn't be quite that simple for me. I would have to work at belonging as an Indian boy never did. I would have to prove I belonged, by being more Arapaho than even the Arapaho themselves.

Chapter Five

AMONG THE ARAPAHO it is a custom that each boy and girl shall have a chum. Usually a boyhood chum remains a lifelong friend. Having none had been one of the things that set me apart. But in the weeks and months that followed, I acquired a chum, perhaps the most unlikely one of all the boys in the band, Two Antelopes.

I suppose he was grateful because I hadn't spilled all that had happened down there on the stream bank. Anyway, while I was sitting outside Red Stone's tepee that day, he came walking up hesitantly and squatted down beside me.

He was taller than I, and thin almost to stringiness. His eyes had a fierce, intent, brooding look about them and his mouth seldom smiled. As often as not he carried some bruise or mark on him from the whippings and beatings Eagle Feather gave him.

Eagle Feather was said to be *haha-ka*, or crazy. *Haha-ka* is the word for moth, which is believed to be crazy because of the erratic way it will fly into a flame to its death. Eagle Feather was not liked in our village, for he was cruel to his two squaws and his son. And because Two Antelopes was moody and sour-tempered, he was said to be like Eagle Feather.

Looking back on it, I can see how strange it was, the way he took to me. He hated the whites fanatically, probably because of the way Eagle Feather mistreated him after a visit from the traders. It was therefore odd that he should take to me, a white, the way he did. Perhaps he felt drawn to me because I was different, apart, as he was. For while Two Antelopes wasn't exactly shunned, neither was he liked, and not only because of his father, but also because of his own surly bad temper.

He looked intently at the sky and said casually, "The *niatha* is now an Arapaho. What is his Arapaho name?"

I said, "Sharp Knife."

"It is a good name." He sat still and silent for a few moments. I kept waiting for him to speak, but he said nothing. I glanced at him and was surprised at the expression in his face. His eyes were narrowed, and the muscles played along his jaw from clenching and unclenching his teeth. Between his knees his fists were clenched until the knuckles showed white.

His voice was strange as he said, "I know a place not far from the village where there are many small rabbits. Get your bow and arrows and we will see who can kill one first."

He waited, motionless, for my answer. He also seemed to be holding his breath.

This was the first real friendship I'd been

shown, except for that offered by Singing Wind, which didn't count because she was a girl. I was taken by surprise. I looked at Two Antelopes and he turned his head to stare at me. Clearly, it was to be friendship or enmity. Two Antelopes' look promised that.

I grinned at him. "All right. As soon as the old men leave, I will get my bow."

The tension went out of him, leaving him loose and relaxed.

After a while the old men came filing out of the tepee. When they had all gone, I went in and got my bow and arrows.

Red Stone did not question me, nor did Beaver Woman. An Arapaho boy is allowed a great deal of freedom and has few responsibilities. Occasionally his father will sit down with him and talk, or will teach him how to do things. Mostly, however, he is allowed to play unmolested, since his play is practice for the things he will do when he is grown.

Two Antelopes and I walked away from the village. The *ga-ahine-na* on the hill called to us, warning us not to go too far.

I recall very clearly the feeling of warmth that filled me that day. The sky was bright, the sun warm upon my bare back. I had a friend. At last I had a friend.

We must have walked several miles. It was the season of *ta-yonei*, or fall. Soon the band would be moving north and east in search of the buffalo. The hunt would last for days, but when it was over there would be meat in every lodge to last the winter, and hides for the women to work upon when the weather was bad.

Creeping carefully and silently, we came to the place where Two Antelopes had said the rabbits were. It was a sort of brushy pocket through the bottom of which ran a small stream. My bow was in my hand, an arrow fitted to the sinew bowstring. I crept along through the grass on my knees and elbows, remembering to stay downwind of the draw.

Two Antelopes had left me, but I could see the tall grass waving off to my right as he crawled through it. He had planned well, for spur-of-the-moment planning, and would come upon the pocket from one end while I came on it from the other.

It seemed forever that I crawled. The dust of the grass and its dry tickle made my skin itch. The sun was hot and I began to sweat. But at last I reached a place from which I could look into the pocket.

Expecting rabbits at most, I was a little shocked to see the two huge beasts that were grazing not fifteen feet from where I lay. One was an enormous old buffalo cow. Her udder was full and low, and nuzzling it hungrily was a big buffalo calf.

I lay still, watching them, not even thinking of trying to kill one. Then all of a sudden it struck me what a big splash I'd make back in the village if I came home with a buffalo. Red Stone would be so proud he could burst, and so would Beaver Woman.

As carefully as I could, I drew back on my bowstring. My arrows were stone-tipped, but they were sharp. I drew the bowstring back until the arrowhead was next to the bow. Aiming carefully and holding my breath, I released the arrow.

Fast and straight the arrow flew, striking the calf in the neck with an audible sound.

The calf bellowed and jerked back from his mother's udder as though it had bitten him. He staggered a few steps, then fell kicking to the ground.

For a moment I couldn't move. When I could, I sprang to my feet and ran toward the calf.

The cow lowered her head, pawed the ground, and bellowed. She would probably have charged had not Two Antelopes come running up at that instant. His face was grinning in a way I'd never seen it before.

Waving our arms, yelling, and making mock charges toward the cow, we drove her off a little ways. She stood, head lowered, rumbling at us and pawing the ground.

Two Antelopes said, "Cut the calf's throat so it will bleed." He was so excited he couldn't stand still. He kept hopping up and down, and stooping to touch the calf. If there was envy in him, it wasn't noticeable.

I got out the knife the Pawnee had tossed to me and cut the calf's throat. Blood gushed onto the ground, pumped by the dying beat of the calf's heart. With shaking hands, Two Antelopes showed me how to open the calf's belly and remove his entrails.

With this done, the carcass was lighter. Two Antelopes took the hind legs and I the front, and we began to drag the animal toward the village.

The sun, hot before, was burning now. Sweat poured off me. Insects flew up from the grass and buzzed angrily around our heads. Flies, drawn by the meat, crawled on our sweaty backs. We dragged, and rested, and dragged again, growing more tired all the time.

The sun dropped to the horizon and fell out of sight. Dusk, cool and softly fragrant, dropped down over the vast plain. We were alone, and yet not alone. We were hunters returning with our kill.

Full dark came, and at last we saw the twinkling fires of the village ahead.

Neither of us had considered leaving the calf and coming back for it, for there was the matter of being believed. A ten-year-old boy doesn't just walk into the village and say, "I killed a buffalo." He brings the carcass and then there is no question that what he says is true.

The minute we came into the village there was a big uproar. Children clustered admiringly around us. Left Hand and Red Stone and Eagle Feather were among the warriors who came to see.

Suddenly I was very proud to be among the Arapaho. I wanted to be one of them. I began to dream of the day when I would be a warrior, and of the great things I would do. I would be like Left Hand, revered and admired by all the people. What I did not know was that my boyhood years would be the last good years of the Arapaho. Already the buffalo were dwindling under the steady pressure of killing.

It is strange what ridiculous things can sometimes affect the whole shape of events. In the land of white men, beaver hats were no longer fashionable, with the result that beaver pelts dropped in price. And because they dropped, the white traders began to demand the tanned and decorated buffalo robes that the Indian women made so well.

And so, for the first time in their history, the plains tribes killed buffalo for hides alone, unwittingly bringing about the start of their own extinction.

Among the Arapaho quite often a father will give away horses or other gifts to celebrate some occasion in his son's life.

One of these occasions is the ear-piercing ceremony. Another is the son's killing of his first big
game.

To celebrate my killing the buffalo calf, Red
Stone presented Left Hand with his finest horse,
his favorite, a large, powerful brown-and-white-
spotted horse.

Riding the horse, Left Hand departed on the
following day, and the village began to make
preparation for the fall buffalo hunt. Scouts, who
had been out for some time, came in to report a
large herd of buffalo some twenty-five miles to
the northeast.

Since the village had been stationary all summer and during the early fall, and because a
village site becomes dirty and smelly after several
months' use, it was decided that the village would
simply move north, closer to the buffalo herd.

Again the tepees came down and again the
loaded travois scratched their twin tracks on the
prairie. The horse herd moved and a huge dust
cloud rose high in the windy, clear air.

For a while Red Stone rode with the village.
Later he would leave and join the hunters, but
now he rode with me. I sat proudly on the horse
he had given me.

Two Antelopes traveled with us, silent, listening as I did to Red Stone's talk. Courteously
Red Stone included Two Antelopes in the
conversation, perhaps realizing I'd made a friend

at last, and glad because I had. Or maybe it was just that Red Stone was naturally kind, and that he understood Two Antelopes' trouble and wanted to help.

Today he did not talk of the customs of the Arapaho, or tell us how to live. Instead, he told stories of his life, the battles he had fought, the coups he had counted.

"When I was sixteen," Red Stone said, "my father decided it was time I went on a war party. Since we had no quarrels with anyone, he planned a horse-stealing foray. We had heard that a Shoshone village about a hundred miles away had many horses and had grown careless because the village was so large.

"First my father invited most of the warriors in the village to take part. They gathered in our lodge, and smoked and talked, and planned the raid.

"We went on horses to a place about five miles from the Shoshone village, and there we left our horses. Afoot, we approached the village in the night, arriving just at dawn, as the horses were being turned out to graze.

"We did not wish to be seen, even by the horse guards, since it is more honorable to steal from an enemy without killing him. So we worked close to the fringe of the herd, and caught horses to ride. Once mounted, we drove off the Shoshone horses, being careful to get them all so that the

Shoshones could not follow. They shot a few arrows at us, but the distance was too great and none of us were hit. And we were lucky, because we had captured all but three or four horses and there was no pursuit."

A simple story, simply told, yet it fired my imagination. I said, "Tell us about your first coup, about the first scalp you took."

Though I didn't realize it at the time, Red Stone had taken my father's place in my life, and now I was listening to his stories as I had to my father's. But my own dreams were the same, of growing up, of doing great things myself.

Red Stone smiled. "I was nineteen. We were hunting in the mountains, myself and two others. We were in the very high country where there are no trees, but only a great many green bushes. We saw a Ute come walking down a hill, also hunting.

"We split up, the two with me circling to right and left, while I went straight toward the Ute. The plan was that we would all reach him at the same time from three different directions.

"Having the shortest distance to cover, and being eager, I reached him first. I rushed him, and struck him in the head with my tomahawk. He fell, and quickly I took his scalp.

"The others came up, and about that time the Ute sat up. He pushed the skin on his forehead and held it up so that he could open his eyes. He looked at us, and then the two with me fell on him and killed him."

Listening to Red Stone's tales, a white man might have been horrified. Theft and murder, he would say. Yet was it? Among the white men's soldiers, it is even an objective to steal from the enemy his means of making war, his supplies, his arms, his horses. Nor is it unusual for white men to take trophies from their vanquished enemies. True, they do not take such grisly trophies. Instead they take guns or knives or parts of uniforms, but the difference is only a difference in custom.

It struck me then, as it has often done since, that in many respects the Indian and his culture are more similar to the white man and his culture than is generally supposed. As it is with the whites, some things about the Indians' way of life is bad. Yet there is much good too.

We proceeded to our new camp site, and by the time we reached it, the hunt was over. All night the hunters streamed into camp, their horses laden with meat and hides.

Almost every particle of the buffalo carcass is used. The meat is eaten, or dried for future use. The bone marrow makes a fine gravy and is also used for softening hides. The hide is used for tepees, for robes, both to wear and to trade, and for moccasins. The shaggy hair of the neck and hump can be woven into strong ropes, used for catching and handling horses. The sinews make bowstrings and thread and sometimes glue. The bladder makes a water skin. Knives and awls and hide scrapers are made from the bones, spoons and ladles from the horns.

Small wonder, then, that the plains tribes became poor when the buffalo became scarce.

For over a week our village was busy from dawn to dark, drying meat, fleshing hides, feasting. The smell of cooking buffalo meat pervaded everything as did the smell of spoilage from the blood and scrap-littered ground. The dogs' bellies protruded as though each of them carried a dozen pups inside, and they now disdained any but the choicest morsels.

This, as all other things, ended. The first snow of winter struck soon after, and the village moved again, this time into the shelter of the foothills along the eastern edge of the great mountains.

As well there was no inner voice to whisper, "Enjoy these years of peace and plenty, Sharp Knife. Enjoy your friends among the Indians. For all things are fleeting. These are the good years. The bad ones are yet to come."

Chapter Six

W ITH MUCH of my inner torment gone, the months and years passed pleasantly, with little to mark them. Fast friends with Two Antelopes, I was his constant companion. We were three, really, for until she was thirteen, Singing Wind was always with us.

Not until later did the conflict between Two Antelopes and myself arise—not until the whites began to sweep the plain like a plague of locusts; not until Singing Wind put on the *to-jehet*, the body wrapping that signifies approaching womanhood.

We rode our stick horses to the buffalo hunt, with some of the boys playing the buffalo, others the hunters. Sometimes we played at being grown in the miniature tepee Singing Wind's mother had made for her. For some reason she always insisted that I be her husband, while Two Antelopes must play at being her brother.

Two Antelopes and I were now permitted to accompany the hunters on buffalo hunts, though we were not allowed to take part for fear we would frighten the huge beasts into flight. Already the buffalo herds were thinning, were becoming more difficult to find.

At other times we would watch from concealed places nearby as Red Stone waited in a specially dug pit, covered with brush and baited with spoiled fish. When the great bald eagles came down for the fish, he would seize them by the legs and kill them for their feathers, ignoring the savage beat of their powerful wings, the cruel raking of their sharp talons.

We learned to rope horses, using ropes made from buffalo hair, their loops held open at the ends by hoops of willow.

For long periods I would forget altogether that I was white. I grew to love the Indians, their gentle ways toward each other. I grew to love the open plain, the easy, free life I led.

Perhaps the only serious thing to mar our life was Eagle Feather, father of Two Antelopes, who became more *haha-ka* as the years passed. He neglected his family, and no longer was his tepee filled with meat. He was often gone from the band, and took to hanging around the white settlements, where he would beg whisky until they grew sick of seeing him around and chased him away. Then he would come home and beat his squaws because they had no robes for him to trade. Red Stone, out of the great goodness of his heart, and perhaps because Two Antelopes was my friend, kept Eagle Feather's tepee supplied with meat while he was gone.

When I was thirteen the white men found gold

in the land far to the west of the mountains, and afterward thousands upon thousands of them swept across the plain in never ending streams. Their lust for the yellow metal was incomprehensible to the Indians, who valued nothing unless it had a clearly defined use.

They brought with them the disease called cholera, named by the Indians "the big cramps," and in 1849 the disease came close to wiping out the Southern Cheyenne.

Disputes and squabbles became frequent between white men and red, largely because neither Indian nor white would consider the others as individuals. If an Indian stole from a white man, vengeance was taken against any Indian. And if a white man injured an Indian, the Indian was no more particular. He took his revenge upon the first white man he caught off guard.

Left Hand, now chief of his own band, preached peace and tolerance, but he was not always heeded, for an Indian is proud, and the whites treated him with lofty contempt and made no attempt to understand his ways.

In the fall of 1849, William Bent destroyed his fort and took Yellow Woman, his Cheyenne wife, and their children down the river to Big Timbers, where he began to build a cabin. Tom Fitzpatrick, the Long Knives' Indian agent, went to stay with Bent, and in November took a sister of Left Hand as his squaw.

There were many gifts from white men to Indian that fall and winter. Comanches and Kiowas, Arapaho and Cheyenne gathered at Big Timbers to receive the gifts.

While we were there I stayed out of sight of the white men, for I had no liking for them. Neither did I want to leave my Indian friends to return to them.

Fitzpatrick was talking a treaty between the whites and the plains tribes so that they might live at peace with each other and so that warfare among the tribes would cease. And Left Hand, now allied with Fitzpatrick by marriage, supported his plan wholeheartedly. He had learned to speak English, so that now when he visited in the tepee of Red Stone he and I talked English exclusively. It was good practice for me, for my English had grown bad from disuse.

But soon we left Big Timbers, having no liking for the overcrowded, stinking village site, and camped for the winter near the foothills. Spring came, and the spring buffalo hunt, and afterward we moved farther eastward on the great plain.

It was that summer that Eagle Feather ran amok, that summer when I was fourteen.

It happened very unexpectedly. Two Antelopes and I were breaking a horse about half a mile from the village. In the distance we saw, with habitually watchful eyes, a single rider approaching from the direction of Big Timbers, to the southwest.

Before long the lone rider became distinguishable to us as Eagle Feather. Two Antelopes broke away at once and ran to the village to warn his mother that Eagle Feather was coming. I followed at a more leisurely pace, arriving just as Eagle Feather entered his tepee.

He was plainly possessed of the belly sickness that follows too much drinking of the white men's medicine water. His eyes were wild and his skin was a grayish, unhealthy color.

He began to bellow at the top of his voice, abusing Two Antelopes and his two squaws. And because there was meat in his tepee that he had not killed himself, he accused his first squaw, the mother of Two Antelopes, of having a lover.

All the village listened uneasily to the loud, quarreling sounds coming from Eagle Feather's tepee, then to the sounds of blows as Eagle Feather began to beat his son, shouting at him to tell who his mother's lover was. After a while Two Antelopes came rolling from the entrance, his mouth bleeding, one of his eyes beginning to swell shut. He looked at me dazedly, then back at the tepee entrance with consuming hatred.

Red Stone came hurrying from our lodge, his face as cold as stone, his eyes hard and angry. Yet he made no move to interfere, since an Indian's reluctance to become involved in a family squabble is even greater than that of a white man.

Inside the tepee, Two Antelopes' mother began to scream and beg. It was a sound that chilled my blood, that made goose pimples stand out on my bare arms and chest. Two Antelopes, beside me, began to shiver violently. He looked beseechingly at Red Stone. "Stop him. Stop him!"

Red Stone took a step toward Eagle Feather's tepee, but he was already too late. Two Antelopes' mother came staggering from the entrance. Her face was a mass of blood beneath the hand she held over it to cover it. From the places where her ears had been, more blood gushed.

Behind her, Eagle Feather burst from the tepee, bloody knife in hand. He screeched with insane fury, "Vulture! Unfaithful one!"

Red Stone stepped over to face him. Red Stone's expression was more terrible than I had ever seen it before. He said in a voice that was cold and still, "You are wrong. You have done a terrible thing to a faithful wife. I was the one that provided meat for your tepee. I did it only from friendship and because you were not here."

Eagle Feather's eyes were wild and irrational. "Then you are the one! I give her to you! You want her so much, then take her! But take her without a nose, without ears, so that everyone shall know what she is and what the two of you have done!"

Before Red Stone could reply, he flung himself to the back of his horse and thundered away.

Beside me, Two Antelopes was still trembling violently. Whispers came from between his tight-clenched teeth. "I'll kill him. I'll follow him and kill him!"

Red Stone beckoned to me. He said harshly, "Go to our tepee and bring Beaver Woman to care for the mother of Two Antelopes."

I ran off at once, but as I left, I could hear Red Stone speaking to Two Antelopes soothingly.

When I returned, both Red Stone and Two Antelopes were gone. Red Stone had taken him away from the village, as he had taken me so many years before. It was now Two Antelopes that needed the wise counseling of Red Stone, Two Antelopes that was mixed up in his mind and needed straightening out.

They were gone all the rest of the day and all through the night. Nighthawk Woman, Two Antelopes' mother, refused to stay in our tepee, as Beaver Woman wished. She was too ashamed. She did not want to look at anyone or see anyone.

It was this shame that cost her her life. For during the night Eagle Feather returned, creeping into the village as silently as a hunting panther. Knife in hand, he entered his tepee and plunged it to the hilt into Nighthawk Woman's breast.

The weeping and screaming of her younger sister, Eagle Feather's other squaw, aroused the village, but it was too late to help Nighthawk

Woman, too late to catch Eagle Feather, who was gone.

The Arapaho have laws regarding murder, but they are less harsh than those of the white man. Had the brother of the dead woman followed and killed Eagle Feather, no blame would have attached to him. Red Stone, as the accused, could also have followed and killed Eagle Feather, and the village would have approved.

But Red Stone did not do so, though he wanted to. He yielded to the fierce insistence of Two Antelopes that Eagle Feather be allowed to live so that someday Two Antelopes himself might kill him.

And so Eagle Feather, without formality but nevertheless by common consent of all the village, became an outcast. No man could sit with him and talk. No one could eat with him. Everything he ate was supposed to taste bad to him. What few horses he still possessed must be given to the relatives of his dead wife. He was, to all intents and purposes, dead himself.

And in one way only could he regain his status as a member of the tribe. He must find an enemy, freshly killed by an Arapaho other than himself, no mean feat in itself. He must then crush the skull of the dead enemy, eat a bit of his brain, taste his blood, break a bone and taste the marrow. He must taste the flesh, a tip of the liver, and a bit of the heart. He must also taste some of the fat from around the heart.

And most important of all, he must do this before eyewitnesses.

There must have been something of my white training remaining to me even after all these years, for when Red Stone related this penance to me I became sick at my stomach. Yet I found it somewhat comforting when Red Stone said, "This is the penance that was taught me by my father, and he by his father before him. Neither I nor my father nor my grandfather ever witnessed or heard of such a penance actually taking place. For murders are rare among our people."

The most disturbing consequence of the murder, so far as I was concerned, was the change that occurred in Two Antelopes.

He had hated the whites before. Now his hatred of them became an obsession, for he blamed the whites even more than he blamed Eagle Feather for his mother's death. It was the white men's medicine water that had driven Eagle Feather *haha-ka*. Therefore upon the white men rested the blame.

I would catch him looking at me strangely, and sometimes thoughtfully fingering the hilt of his knife. I could not fail to know that he was thinking of me not as Sharp Knife, his friend, but as a member of the hated white race. Oddly enough, I found myself, who disliked the whites, cast in the unwitting role of their defender.

Two Antelopes fought his age, the slowness of his growing up. But he was now seventeen, and would soon be of an age when he could be a warrior.

"Another year," he would breathe in an oddly tense voice. "Another year and I will be able to make war upon them. I will kill every white I see, until they know Two Antelopes as a scourge even worse than the big cramps."

And I would say stubbornly, "Two Antelopes, wise as he is and brave as he is, makes the same mistake the white men make. He lumps the whites, good and bad, into one group, and calls all of them bad. Two Antelopes' war is with the traders who sell the medicine water to the Arapaho."

He'd look at me fiercely. "Does Sharp Knife remember that white blood flows in his veins? Does he ally himself with our enemies and thus become the enemy of Two Antelopes? Does he forget our friendship?"

There was no answer that Two Antelopes would accept save for, "I also hate the whites. I hate them for stealing the land of the Arapaho, for scattering and killing the buffalo so that every year the hunt becomes more difficult. I hate them for poisoning our warriors with medicine water and for violating our mothers in their lodges. I hate them for their arrogance and because they hold us in contempt."

This answer I gave him many times, yet always he accepted it grudgingly and with reservations.

The summer passed, and winter passed, but the tension between Two Antelopes and myself did not decrease. Less and less were we together now, and more often was I alone.

Singing Wind, wearing the *to-jehet*, was kept busy in her home, learning how to cook and tan hides and sew in preparation for marriage, and I saw little of her. But always when we passed I would feel her eyes upon me furtively, and if I would meet her glance, she would smile shyly.

For some reason, her smiles and glances stirred a strange excitement in me, an excitement I did not fully understand at the time. Singing Wind was the one that had romped and played with us these many years. Why then should the sight of her stir me so now?

The *to-jehet* and the blanket she wore failed to conceal her changing form entirely. She was filling out like fruit ripening upon a tree. Nor was I the only one that noticed the change. Two Antelopes took to hanging around within sight of Singing Wind's tepee too, and the tension between us became even greater.

When fresh grass began to green the plain, when the bushes bloomed and new bright leaves covered the trees, the trader Sonofabitch Smith again visited our village. In late evening he came, as always, and with him were the same two that had been with him before.

Out at the edge of the village they pitched their camp, with the braves of our village clustered around watching them like hungry dogs. The wooden kegs were unlashed from the mules' backs and set upon the ground. The top of one was knocked out.

Even Red Stone, wise, kind Red Stone, had no resistance to the liquor, and he was among those that waited with an almost groveling patience for their first drink of the strong, foul whisky.

I had not realized how much I had grown until I saw the white men. I discovered now with some surprise that I was nearly as tall as Sonofabitch Smith himself. My shoulders were broad and muscular, and in color my skin was like that of the Arapaho. My black hair was done in braids that hung halfway to my waist, one on each side. An eagle feather was stuck in my hair and in my ears I wore a pair of turquoise earrings that Red Stone had bartered from a passing Comanche, who had in turn stolen them from a dead Navaho. Made of dark turquoise, they matched almost perfectly the color of my eyes.

Already a beard was beginning to grow upon my face. Now it was but a fuzz, fine and straggly, but I knew that soon, if I were to continue to look like an Arapaho, I would have to start shaving.

Red Stone had tried pulling out each hair as it grew, but besides being painful, it proved a useless, endless task, for as though trying to replace each hair pulled out, two more grew in.

I was Sharp Knife the Arapaho, who already was casting sheep's eyes at Singing Wind, who even now was slipping away from the village at night to learn to play the *kakush*, a flute made of wood, fringed with buckskin and held together with buckskin bands. Painted ocher red, it is used by courting swains for serenading their sweethearts. I was not of an age to marry, but custom cannot still the heat that stirs a young man's loins, cannot deaden the timeless demands the soft eyes of a maiden stir in his heart.

Tonight, instead of being sent to Red Stone's tepee, I stood at the edge of the village and watched with disgust and no longing the process of men being turned into animals without dignity as they drank of the fiery liquid in Sonofabitch Smith's wooden kegs.

The process of trading would be no different tonight, I knew, than it had been in the past. In the morning the traders would leave, burdened heavily with fine buffalo robes, leaving nothing behind but a few worthless trinkets and some of their even more worthless seed in the bellies of our Indian women. Anger stirred me as I watched, and an ever growing hatred for the whites.

I was perhaps the only one that saw Sonofa-bitch slip away. Even I did not see the reason for his leaving until I began to follow. Then I saw the slim, pliant figure of Singing Wind, heading for the stream with a water skin. Suddenly I remembered the hot, red, lustful eyes of Sonofabitch Smith that night so long ago as he had gazed at our village.

Silent as a shadow, I slipped after him. My fingers fondled the handle of the Pawnee knife at my belt. It was the knife from which my name derived.

Singing Wind disappeared from sight in the willows that lined the bank of the stream. The murmur of the water reached me, and the gurgling sound of it entering the mouth of her water skin. In my mind I could see her kneeling there, a slim ankle, showing beneath the fringe of her skirt. I could see the smooth swell of hip and thigh, revealed by her tightened skirt as she knelt. I could see the round, proud fullness of her breasts, thrusting against her deerskin dress, her gleaming hair, her soft, smooth skin and big, gentle eyes.

These things I saw in my mind, but Sonofabitch Smith saw them in the flesh, for I could hear his hoarse, lustful breathing ahead of me as he watched.

A twig cracked beneath his feet, and I knew he had moved. I knew that now he was approaching her, as silent, as menacing as the panther bent on a kill.

Heavy he was, big and clumsy as a bear. But he was also a man of the mountains and the plains. He had kept his hair these many years trading in the land of Comanche and Sioux, of Apache and Arapaho. He was a man not to be taken lightly, or to be attacked carelessly. On silent moccasins I crept closer so as not to warn him of my approach.

The water stopped gurgling into the water skin. Easing through the willows, I saw Singing Wind rise to her feet, the water skin bulky in her hands. I saw Sonofabitch waiting nearby, waiting until she should pass him and he could grasp her from behind, muffle her outcry with one hand while he tore the clothes from her with the other.

I moved quickly. With a leap I was upon him, my arm encircling his throat, choking off the harsh yelp that sprang to his lips.

Singing Wind's cry of alarm was soft and quick, scarcely more than a swiftly indrawn breath.

He fought like the grizzly. The point of the Pawnee knife entered his back, but before it could pierce his vitals, he stopped and flung me over his head. My iron grasp on his throat was broken. Like a doll thrown by an angry girl child, I flew through the air and landed in midstream with a tremendous splash.

"Sonofabitch!" he yelled, forgetting Singing

Wind altogether in the pain of the knife wound in his back.

I shouted, "Run, Waanibe! Run to your lodge. You will be safe, for I will kill this one."

She ran, but Sonofabitch only laughed. "Kill me, will ye? Why, goddamn ye, I'll eat yer gizzard. I'll drink yer blood!"

I got to my feet in the shallow water. I could see the gleam of a knife in Sonofabitch's hand.

I waded toward him, feeling the cold touch of fear for the first time. The thing that had fed my fury, Singing Wind's danger, was gone now, and I knew I faced a fight more dangerous than the one I had faced years before as Two Antelopes drew the tomahawk from his breechclout.

Why I lapsed into English I don't know. Perhaps it was because Sonofabitch was using it even while his mind translated what I'd said from the Arapaho.

My voice came from between teeth that chattered from the wetness and the cold. "I'm the one that's goin' to kill you, mister. You've peddled your last cup of whisky in this village. You've slept with your last Arapaho woman."

The sound of English, good old St. Louis English, coming from the lips of an Indian boy must have been a considerable shock to him. His mouth fell open and he wheezed, "Well, I'll be a sonofabitch! You a white kid, sonny?"

"My skin's white, but I reckon that's all. I'm as

Indian as any. You feel the edge of this knife in your guts an' you'll know I'm Indian."

Sonofabitch began to back off right then. He said in a wheedling voice, "Now come off it, sonny. I didn't tetch the leetle gal. I was only aimin' to steal a kiss, anyhow."

"Liar!"

"All right. So mebbe I did want more. But I didn't git it an' there ain't no reason to stay riled up, is there?"

He'd been backing away all the time, and suddenly he was lost to my sight in the willows. I heard him crashing through them, and then silence.

Whether he'd got through them, or whether he was waiting in there for me, I didn't know. But suddenly I knew I wasn't going to find out. I might as well admit it. I wasn't a warrior yet.

But I would be. Before long I would be. And then perhaps I could right some of the wrongs being done to the Indians.

Left Hand preached patience and understanding. Two Antelopes demanded extermination. Which way I would choose only time could tell.

That night Sonofabitch Smith tried to talk Red Stone into sending me back with him. And Red Stone, for once, refrained from more drinking, because he sensed that this was a crisis.

He called me into the tepee where Sonofabitch was, nursing a sore, stiff back, and asked me whether I wished to go with the white man or stay with him.

Of course I said I'd stay with him. I said I was an Arapaho and would always be an Arapaho. I doubt if I'll ever forget the look that came into his eyes then. They were grateful, and humble, and everlastingly glad.

II. THE MAN

Chapter Seven

IN MAY of the following year, 1850, a messenger came to our village bringing word from Tom Fitzpatrick at Big Timbers that he had many gifts for his friends the Arapaho, and asking them to attend a conference at which his treaty was to be discussed. Shortly thereafter another messenger came from Left Hand, also asking us to attend.

The long awaited peace with the white men was near. All the plains tribes were supposed to attend, Comanche, Apache, Kiowa, Shoshone, Pawnee, Arapaho, Cheyenne, Sioux, traditional enemies and traditional friends to meet on the same ground and smoke the same pipe.

Our village packed up and the travois scratched their way south. With Left Hand's village we camped, and as more came in they set up around us, Cheyenne and Arapaho both, until we numbered several thousand. But the others did not come in. "Too many enemies," they said, "for a peace conference."

Through the villages moved the white soldiers,

laughing, joking, learning bits of our language and flirting with the women, being scowled upon by some among our men.

There were no incidents save one. But that one threatened to turn the whole peace conference into an all-out war.

A young Cheyenne chief saw a ring upon the finger of an officer's wife. Curious, he seized her hand and took the ring off to look at it. Were not the Indians and the white men friends? And was there harm in simply looking?

Apparently there was. The frightened woman screamed and her husband appeared with a buggy whip. Thinking the Cheyenne was molesting his wife, he lashed the young chief across the face.

A deadly insult, erasable only in blood. Temper boiled through the villages. Chiefs and medicine men galloped back and forth, crying for the tribes to avenge themselves. The white men could molest Indian women at will, but let an Indian touch a white woman, even out of curiosity, and immediate retaliation was the result.

War was averted by Left Hand and some of the cooler chiefs among the Cheyenne, and by William Bent and Tom Fitzpatrick, who were profuse with their apologies.

Sullenly the Cheyenne accepted their gifts and left. And we departed too, promising to return in the fall for the actual signing.

The summer passed pleasantly enough, though

hunting was hard. And still the whites streamed across the plain, as Left Hand's dream had told him they would.

In the fall we went again to Big Timbers, and this time all the tribes were there, more than ten thousand strong. Herds of horses grazed the plain as far as the eye could see.

The treaty was signed after much delay. It gave the Arapaho, Cheyenne, and Sioux all the land between the Arkansas and the North Platte, and ceded to the whites the right to use the travel routes and to build forts.

A fair enough treaty, we thought, not knowing that it would hold only until the whites needed more. Then there must be another treaty and another, each one giving them more of our lands, until at last they would have them all.

With peace existing between Indian and white, and also between traditional enemies among the tribes, we gave our time to hunting and forsook the pursuit of war. It was well that we did, for only by continuous hunting were we now able to keep our lodges supplied with meat.

And each year, because we were growing poor, we traveled to Big Timbers for the white men's gifts of food, clothing, and ammunition. No longer were we a proud people, dependent only upon ourselves. We needed the white men now, and were dependent upon their bounty.

I heard Two Antelopes time and again haranguing a group of young men. "We have become a race of beggars, crawling to Big Timbers for the white men's gifts. And why do we need their gifts? Because they have killed and scattered the game upon which we once lived. Kill them, I say! Kill them all or drive them from our lands! When we have done that, then the game will return and once again the Arapaho can hold up their heads and be proud."

On his periodic visits to our village, Left Hand, having more and more influence among the Southern Arapaho, continued to advocate peace.

And so the years passed.

Being young, with my blood running hot, I was less interested in the future than I was in the business of growing up, of day-to-day living. I sat beside Red Stone and stared at the fire while he taught me the courting and marriage customs of the Arapaho. "You are too young to take a bride," he said, "though the heat is in your loins and the fire of manhood burns in your heart. The tribe needs its young men as warriors, unhindered by the ties of marriage and family. I was not married until I was thirty, and that is the usual age, though a girl may marry when she is fifteen."

Fifteen. And Singing Wind was sixteen. Already the warriors were playing the kakush before her father's tepee. Already they loitered along the path she must take to the stream, waiting like sheep for the glance from her that would tell them they might speak. They pestered her brother, asking for her as a wife, and they sought his favor as desperately as they sought hers.

I said, "I want Singing Wind for my wife. I cannot wait until I am thirty, for by then she will be taken in marriage."

"You must wait. You will find another as fair as Singing Wind."

A feeling of desperation came over me. Eleven years. I must wait for eleven years. I must watch while another took Singing Wind to his tepee. I must lie at night with the fire burning in my loins, and dream of Singing Wind in my arms. I must feel the tension grow in me until I could think of nothing else. And nowhere could I find relief, not in Singing Wind or in any other woman of the tribe. For the standard of virtue among the Arapaho is high. There are no prostitutes.

Red Stone understood my need, and smiled sadly. "These times are hard for a young man," he said. "In the old days, the young warriors who had no wives would make a raid upon an enemy village. They would steal a woman who was out picking berries alone. They would satisfy their need with her and then release her. Or perhaps they would kill her, depending upon the way they felt, and how willing she was. But all that is changed. We are at peace now."

As well that we were. For I would never accept this solution to my problem. Enough of my white training remained to force its rejection.

I was angry but did not know exactly why. I got up and left the tepee. I wandered through the darkness, struggling to grasp some elusive thought that lingered at the edge of my consciousness.

Suddenly I had it. I remembered my mother's being carried away screaming by half a dozen young Arapaho braves. And I knew at last how she had died.

Walking, I left the village behind and wandered out across the dark, vast plain. Knowing what I knew, could I live among the murderers of my mother? Could I accept as brothers the very ones who had raped and killed her, even though I did not know their names?

Even yet I remember the stark horror of that night. My thoughts beat against my skull until it ached with a terrifying intensity. I trembled and sweated and shook with chill. I fell to the ground and beat upon it with my fists.

I hated the Arapaho as I had never hated the whites. Their kindness to me was a cruel farce. Their ways were hateful. They were cruel and lustful savages, with no decency in them.

These things I thought, and these things I knew to be untrue even as I thought them.

Morning found me far from the village. I

do not know how many miles it was, five, ten, twenty. I had not quieted my inner torment, but only seemed to have increased it. Indian or white, which was I to be? Must I return to the whites, whom I despised? Must I return to the red murderers who had killed my mother? Or must I forever wander alone, neither red nor white, rejecting both and rejected by both?

I became hungry, but I had no weapons save for the Pawnee knife. I thought of trying to kill something to eat with it. And then suddenly I remembered Left Hand, his tale of the vision he'd seen during a fast.

I was nineteen now. I was old enough to fast. Perhaps in fasting I would see the face of God myself, and he would tell me what to do. He would quiet the awful torment of my mind, put me at peace within myself. He would say either "Return to the whites" or "Go back to Red Stone, your father, to Singing Wind, your sweetheart, to the Arapaho, your brothers."

I looked around me and discovered I was near the foothills. A long ridge lay ahead of me, the hogback that divides the plain from the mountains.

I climbed to the top of this, and there found a great pile of huge rocks. At the very top of this pile I found a hollowed-out rock on which I could stretch full length and sleep.

I was tired and near to exhaustion. I fell down

on the warm surface of the rock, kept from rolling off by its cradle-like depression, and promptly went to sleep.

My thinking was predominantly Arapaho that day, for I had chosen the Arapaho way of talking with God, of settling the confusion of my soul. The white way would have been to seek a priest, a minister, and find solace in his counsel.

I awoke, and stared at the blazing sun, which drew the sweat from my body until it soaked my deerskin clothes, until it dripped from my naked chest. I looked away from the sun, but everywhere I looked I still saw it as though it were etched into my very eyeballs.

Thirst was a ravening hunger within me. My tongue swelled and my mouth was dry as dust. I was hungry, for I had not eaten in nearly twenty-four hours. Yet this was but the first day. Most fasts lasted three, some as long as seven days.

Could I stand it for seven days? I didn't know. I could only try.

My mind wearied of its tortured thoughts and put them aside. I watched the white, puffy clouds drift lazily across the turquoise sky. I watched an eagle, sailing majestically at a height that made him appear but a speck, and saw him plummet to earth with his wings folded until he was a bullet fired from Chiva Niatha's musket.

A mountain sheep leaped to my rock, saw me, and nearly plunged to his death in sudden surprise and his effort to get away. A rattlesnake crawled over a rock nearby, looked at me with his beady, unblinking eyes, and slithered hurriedly away.

An omen already? Was this Ha-sananen's way of telling me I was to be shunned by Indian and white alike?

"Wait," I said aloud. "It is still too soon." My voice sounded cracked and reedy, not like my own.

At last the night came, and I slept again. But this night was cold, and I woke shivering violently. My teeth chattered. My flesh was like ice. I was hungry to desperation, so thirsty I thought I would surely die, and growing weak and lightheaded.

Bi-gushish, the moon, was up, a quarter moon now in the western sky. Its light reflected on the shining surface of the twisting stream at the foot of the hogback.

I weakened. This fasting was but a barbaric Indian custom, and I hated the Indians. I would give up this fast, walk down to that stream, and bury my face in its cool depths. I would let it run down my throat until my ravening thirst was dead, until I could drink no more. Then I would hunt until I had killed some meat, or would feast upon wild berries.

But I did not rise. Some force over which I had no control seemed to hold me there.

Gray stained the eastern horizon. Shivering,

I watched the glory of pink and purple and orange staining the sky, and, warming, I watched Hishinishish, the day sun, begin the long climb to his high perch above the world.

To the eastward stretched the plain, rolling, brown with high, dry grasses until it lost itself in the haze of infinity. I felt my strength and will return, though the light feeling in my head did not go away. I would stay, and would fast for as long as was necessary. I would see the face of God and listen to His words.

To take my mind from my hunger, I watched the small insects crawling on the ground about me, and felt a kinship with them. Ants paraded in an army at the foot of my perch, for all the world like the streams of white men pouring across the land of the Arapaho. They bore burdens upon their backs, and disappeared from sight around the corner of a rock.

I watched a horned toad sunning himself, and stared back at a rock lizard that approached and stared at me curiously.

My body grew warm and the chill of the night subsided. But there was to be no comfort, for the sun beat upon me mercilessly until again I sweated away the moisture of my body, until again my mouth grew dry as though it were filled with feathers.

I thought of Singing Wind, her eyes like the dove's, her lips soft and full and smiling. There was no heat, no urgency in my thoughts of her today. Instead, I knew a longing of the spirit more intense than any longing of the body can ever be.

Could I bear to leave her and return to the whites?

Memory of my father and mother had faded through the years. I found that my mind could no longer picture either of them. Instead, when I thought of the whites it was a vision of Sonofabitch Smith that rose to my mind, coarse, lustful, whiskered, and smelly, as though he had forgotten what the clear water of the stream was for.

And yet, even if I remained with the Arapaho, I would lose Singing Wind. I would lose her in a way more painful than seeing her killed. For she would be taken in marriage by some warrior of the tribe. She would go to his lodge, and swell with his child. She would lie with him in the fragrant night, straining against him, while I would sleep alone, tense with longing.

I forced my thoughts to leave me. The time was not yet. Ha-sananen was not yet ready to reveal himself.

This day dragged far more slowly than the previous one. It was endless. My lips cracked and I could not swallow. My eyes burned from the sun's glare. My belly cramped until I doubled over and groaned with pain. My skin became sore and red from the fiery rays of the sun.

And again I looked at the coolness of the stream below me, again weakening, but I did not leave my perch.

A small band of antelope crossed the plain before me, mere specks because of their distance. A single old buffalo bull lumbered along with them, as though he could find none of his own kind and would not stay alone.

Was this the omen for which I waited? Was I the old buffalo bull? Were the antelope the Arapaho, with whom I must stay?

Weakness overcame me. I sank down upon the hot rock. The world whirled about before my eyes. Scarcely feeling the burning rock on my naked chest, I went to sleep.

It could hardly be called sleep, for it was much akin to death. I had no dreams and knew nothing. I was like one drugged with medicine water, and the hours fled past.

Nightfall came but I did not know it.

In the middle of the night I awoke. I sat up and stared around me. The air was chill, but I was not cold. My head felt as though it floated somewhere above the earthbound clay of my body.

I heard a voice, like the distant rumble of thunder. A chill ran across my body, but it was not a chill caused by cold.

The voice said, "Sharp Knife the Arapaho, I have been waiting for you."

I felt humble and small, and dared not speak.

Would I see God, as Left Hand had, and would He look the same?

Almost afraid to look, I stared around. I saw only the night, heard only the breezes whispering past the barren rocks.

The voice spoke again. "Your skin is white, but your spirit is that of the Arapaho. Return to them. Would you refuse the chokecherry because it has a seed? Nothing is all good, Sharp Knife. The summer is but sweeter because of the bitter cold of winter. Food is only the better after a man has known the pangs of hunger. Take heart. Singing Wind will not go to the tepee of another."

Again there was a long silence, and only the breezes and the far distant cry of a wolf broke its completeness.

I was like a child yearning toward its mother's breast. I hungered for more of this calm, strong wisdom. Yet I did not speak.

The voice came again. "Live as you must, Sharp Knife. Revere the good in all men and do not condemn when you see the bad. Nothing is easy, nor will your life be easy. There will be much war, and many will die. But the whites are like a flood and nothing can hold them back. Understand them, and teach them to understand you."

The voice died away into nothingness as a rumble of summer thunder dies.

I could not move. I had not the strength. Yet I knew no fear. I would somehow find my way back to the village. I would have the strength for that.

I slept again, and when I awoke it was to the warm rays of the sun against my body. Rising, I climbed carefully down from the rock. When I tried to walk, I fell. So I began to crawl downward toward the stream.

Strong hands lifted me and offered me water from a water skin. I rested, and when my eyes could see I saw Red Stone sitting nearby. He was watching me, the deep lines of his face tracing a pattern of sadness and tenderness.

"You have fasted," he said. "Now you must eat."

He did not question me about my fast, nor did he ask if I had seen a vision.

I ate a little of the pemmican he offered me, and drank more water. After a while the strength began to flow back into my body. I felt cleansed, as though by fire, and strong again in my mind.

Red Stone asked, "Will you return to the Arapaho, or will you go to the whites?"

"I will go with you, Neisa-na."

At the foot of the hogback were two horses. Together we rode east.

I did not question Red Stone's finding me, for I knew how he had done it. He had trailed me patiently from the village, and had waited out the days and nights of my fast in some unseen place nearby.

Perhaps the wait had been harder for Red Stone than it had been for me. But gladness was a glow in his dark eyes, a smile upon his wide mouth, and I knew he would say that having me return was worth the wait.

Chapter Eight

INEVITABLY, the peace of 1851 was broken. Perhaps the beginning of it was in 1854, when Utes, who had not signed the treaty, attacked and wiped out a fort west of Big Timbers called Pueblo.

There followed trouble with the Sioux over a thing so ridiculous that it was sickening. A Sioux killed an old, lame cow belonging to a white man of the faith called Mormon. The whites raised an outcry, and the Sioux chiefs offered ten dollars as indemnity. The white man demanded twenty-five. The quarrel dragged out, with neither side giving ground. The upshot of it was that a Long Knife lieutenant named Grattan marched out of Fort Laramie to teach the Sioux a lesson. The Sioux killed him and every man with him.

The cause of the original quarrel was now forgotten. Nor did it matter which Sioux warriors had killed the lieutenant and his men. As was so tragically common in disputes between Indians and whites, blame was laid on the whole Sioux nation. So, seeking vengeance, a Colonel Harney was sent out with a large detachment. They attacked, with no justification, a peaceful village of Sioux who had probably not even heard of the

Mormon cow or of Lieutenant Grattan. They tried to flee, offering no resistance. But Harney was determined to kill some Sioux. He slaughtered eighty-six, most of them women and children.

The Cheyenne came next—the Northern Cheyenne. A Long Knife officer demanded some horses from a passing band, claiming they belonged to the whites. Perhaps they did. Reasonably the Cheyenne surrendered three, claiming a fourth belonged to them.

The officer arrested three of them, who then tried to escape. Two were shot to death, the third imprisoned.

The band fled north to the Black Hills, where, to avenge themselves, they killed a trapper who had not even heard of the horses or of the original trouble.

And now one incident led to another, until among whites and Indians alike the feeling was strong that the other was deliberately provoking war.

In May of the year following my fast, and when I was twenty, large-scale trouble again flared between the whites and the Cheyenne.

The same Harney who had slaughtered the Sioux village routed a party of Cheyenne and destroyed their village, a large one numbering 171 lodges.

Destitute, without homes or food, they found refuge among other Cheyenne, and among the

Arapaho, their friends. A number of families came to our village, where they were quartered and fed. Our women helped make new tepees for them, and resupplied them with clothing. Our men, of which I was one, hunted with them so that they would have meat in their new lodges.

Their anger was great, and they spoke out savagely against the whites. The white men did not want peace, they said. The whites had deliberately violated the treaty, which had allowed them to build forts, but not towns and settlements. White men were settling from one end of the land to the other, building cabins, plowing land. Where there had been one travel route before there were now half a dozen.

Two Antelopes was as fiery in his denunciation of the whites as the most rabid among them. And when they left, he departed with them. He did not tell me good-by, but only gave me a sour, level stare as he rode stiff-backed from the village.

I knew what he was thinking—that no longer would he listen to talk of peace. Now he could hear the talk he wanted. War talk. Probably he was telling himself that the Arapaho were women, afraid to fight the whites.

It was not true. We were not afraid. But we had signed a treaty with the whites, and so far as the Arapaho were concerned, it had not been broken.

The summer passed, and fall came. The winter

howled down out of the north, covering the plain with snow, filling the streams with ice so that a man must chop a hole in it before he could drink.

Even when I was not occupied with hunting, I had avoided Singing Wind, for I knew the futility of courtship. Yet there were times when my longing for her became so great that I could scarcely stand it. Two Antelopes was gone, and besides, he was no longer my friend. Red Stone was older than I, and so was Left Hand. I needed someone to talk with—someone my own age or near it. I needed Singing Wind.

So one night I slipped from our lodge and went quietly and unseen through the village until I came to the lodge of Gray Cloud, her father. The wind was from the north, and the flap at the tepee peak was arranged so that it sheltered the smoke hole from the wind and permitted the smoke to be drawn out of the lodge. Smiling with anticipation, I changed the setting so that the flap funneled the wind directly into the hole.

I had not long to wait. From within the tepee I heard Gray Cloud coughing. "Waanibe, go outside and fix the smoke flap."

She came quickly from the tepee, grasped the pole, and adjusted the flap. She would have returned, but I caught the sleeve of her robe and placed a hand upon her mouth.

"Quiet. It is I, Sharp Knife."

Instantly her body became as still as death.

She looked up at me, her eyes enormous, dark, reflecting the sparkle of a thousand stars.

I said, "I must see you, Waanibe. I must talk to you. My life is winter without you."

Her breathing was rapid, and I could see the rise and fall of her breasts in the cold starlight.

She breathed, "I must go back. They will worry."

I whispered hastily, "I will be up the stream where the large cottonwood tree has fallen tomorrow in the early morning. Will you come?"

Her answer was a quick pressure on my arm. And then she was gone.

I went down to Red Stone's tepee and lay down to sleep, but sleep would not come. Every time I closed my eyes I saw Singing Wind in my mind.

Tomorrow she would come to me. Surely she would come.

Somehow the night passed. Toward morning I slept a little, and dreamed that Gray Cloud found us together and forbade our seeing each other again.

I awoke in a sweat of fear. Suppose that did happen? What would we do?

I ate quickly and hurried out. I went to the stream and bathed, then returned to the tepee, where I decorated my face with red ocher mixed with buffalo tallow. It is thought among the whites that red paint on an Indian's face means that he is on the warpath. It is not true. The Arapaho decorates his face with red paint whenever he is under the spell of some excitement. It may be war, but it may also be love.

I dressed in my best clothes, went through the village and upstream to the fallen cottonwood.

I waited for what seemed an eternity. Then, toward the village, I heard a twig snap.

Singing Wind was coming toward me, her body lithe as a willow wand, her eyes wide and frightened, yet expectant and glad too. I did not know what to say, nor did she. At last I said, "Waanibe, I am not old enough to take a wife. But I want no other but you. If you marry I shall never take a wife."

She looked as she had that day so long ago when she was a little girl, standing firm but watching me with frightened eyes. She murmured, "I shall wait for you, Sharp Knife, for I have loved you all my life."

I said, "When I fasted in the rocks at the top of the long ridge, Ha-sananen came to me and told me you would wait."

"Then how could it be otherwise?"

I felt triumph and excitement rising in my body. I stepped toward her and she did not move. I took her in my arms and looked down into her eyes. They shone like a thousand stars. Yet they were afraid, too. Arapaho custom is strict regarding a young girl of the marriage age. She is not supposed to be alone with any young man.

Quite plainly Singing Wind was thinking of this. But it was also plain that she would do whatever I asked, custom or not.

I bent down and kissed her on the cheek. It was soft and smooth, warm beneath my lips. Her body began to tremble.

Arapaho often kiss and embrace when welcoming a loved one from a long absence, but they do not kiss the mouth of another. Steeped in Arapaho customs as I was, still I remembered that my mother and father had kissed each other's lips.

Singing Wind's were like the petals of a flower, moist and soft and inviting. I touched them with my own.

Suddenly she was crushed within my arms. Her body, like that of a caught bird, fluttered and struggled a moment, trying desperately to escape. Then it surrendered to me with a passion that matched my own.

I could take her here, now, and she would never regret it. She would be mine for as long as I lived. Yet I knew, even while my head roared and the blood raced through my body, that it was wrong. Perhaps Singing Wind would not regret it. But I would. I would regret hurting her, lowering her in the eyes of her family, the village, herself.

I pushed her away and held her at arm's length. "Singing Wind, I will love you as long as there is breath in my body. If you wait, I will take you to my tepee, you alone, for I shall never take but one wife. Until then, my *kakush* will make soft music outside the lodge of your father. When you go to the stream for water, I will pluck at your robe, and when you stop we will talk. When I can no longer endure being without you, I shall change the smoke flap at the top of Gray Cloud's tepee, and when you come out I will take you in my arms."

She smiled, and her eyes were glad.

I said, "No hunter among the Arapaho shall find and kill more meat than Sharp Knife. I shall be honored and praised throughout the land, and you will be proud of me."

"I am already proud of Sharp Knife. He is kind, and honest, and loyal to his friends the Arapaho. I am proud to be his chosen one."

Back toward the village a shrill voice rose. "Waanibe! Come here, you lazy girl! There is work to be done!"

Singing Wind smiled. "I must go. My heart will wait for your coming, my body for your embrace." She flushed. "My lips will await your kisses, Sharp Knife, for they make me feel very loving inside."

Then she was gone.

Ambition fired me. A pity we were not at war. I wanted to take my lance and bow, the Pawnee knife and my fastest horse. I wanted to ride to the villages of our enemies and take many scalps, which I would bring home in triumph. I wanted to make Singing Wind very proud of me.

But we were not at war, so that was not possible. I returned to the village and caught my horse. I rode out, determined to begin building a name for myself as a great hunter.

I hunted all day and saw no game. All the next day I also hunted, with like results. The third day I killed a small female antelope, part of which I presented to Gray Cloud.

Others among us were not so fortunate as I. They hunted without success for fresh meat while they used up the dried meat they had laid aside for the winter. Some even cooked raw hides and ate them, which is not quite as desperate a measure as it sounds, since they can be very palatable.

But as the days passed, the situation worsened instead of growing better. The game seemed to have almost disappeared from the plain.

None of us should have been surprised. We had seen this coming for many snows. Yet it seemed that one day there had been game upon the prairie and the next it was gone.

I wondered if Ha-sananen were punishing me for my boastfulness, for my breach of custom in asking Singing Wind to come to me alone. I discarded the idea almost at once. The God of the Arapaho would not punish all the Arapaho for a mistake made by a single member of their tribe.

No, it was the whites that were to blame. The whites alone.

The summer wore away, and fall passed. In our village was hunger and want. We shared our dried meat and berries, our winter provisions, until they were gone. I grew haggard from too little food, from too much riding and hunting. A cottontail or a grouse was a successful day's bag.

Singing Wind was all that sustained me. I would go to her tepee at night and change the setting of the smoke flap, and she would come out to me.

I believe Gray Cloud knew she was seeing me, and I am sure he disapproved. For he knew he could, by permitting her to marry one of her other suitors, enrich himself by many horses and robes. Yet he said nothing. His love for Singing Wind, his only girl child, was great, and deep within himself he desired for her only what she desired herself.

She would come out and we would stand close together, quietly talking, giving strength to each other by our closeness and love. And I would go away with my resolve strengthened.

But resolve could not bring back the game. It could not put meat in the pot when there was no meat. Red Stone grew very thin and developed a hacking cough. Beaver Woman also grew thin.

Throughout the village, children cried because they were hungry.

No longer did our people go to the stream each morning to bathe. They became listless and dirty, and they did not seem to care.

At last, in early winter, the old men of the village, with Red Stone among them, held a council in the tepee of the sacred pipe, and it was decided that the band would go to the white settlement called Denver. We would camp upon its outskirts, and because we were hungry, our white brothers would feed us. In return we would give them what fur peltries we had been able to trap, and what buffalo robes remained in our lodges.

In addition, the wise men of our village thought, we would learn the ways of the white men, and they our ways. We would become fast friends with them, and they with us. We would prove what Chief Left Hand had told us, that by learning to live with the whites we could all survive.

We packed our belongings on travois and started north. There was renewed hope and great excitement in all the people. But in me was a leaden despair. I knew they were being too hopeful. I told myself I knew the whites.

The whites would not care that we were hungry. They would see us only as savages—dirty savages, at that. They would look upon us with contempt. Because there were few women among them, they would lust after our women, and would bring medicine water to the village to trade for their favors.

Suddenly I remembered the prophetic words of Left Hand; "They will lie with our women while we squat before our tepees and offer no protest."

"Never!" Red Stone had said. I thought of Singing Wind, and repeated the word to myself: "Never!"

Chapter Nine

I WAS AMAZED at the size of the settlement they called Denver. Even from a distance, it seemed to sprawl out over a tremendously large area. I guessed there must have been nearly two hundred buildings.

Its streets teemed with activity. Huge freight wagons drawn by several spans of horses crawled through the deep dust on their apparently aimless errands. There were carriages and buggies and men on horseback in abundance. Women, garbed in silks and carrying parasols against the rays of the sun, moved daintily along the walks. Seeing them, I felt uncouth and savage and incredibly dirty.

Our arrival created a minor panic, for it was thought at first that we were bent on war. How the whites could have thought that passes belief, for we had our lodges, our women and children, even our dogs with us. We wore no paint.

While we were still several miles away, three horsemen approached at a gallop. They were dressed in buckskins, and looked much like the traders who had been with Sonofabitch Smith. Their leader spoke to our chief, who wore the ceremonial feather headdress, in the Arapaho tongue.

"Welcome. Our people are honored at your visit. But they are apprehensive that you have come for war and have sent us to see."

Our chief, White Otter, said, "Would we bring our lodges and our children if we came for war? No. We come to visit our brothers the white men. We came to trade, for game is scarce upon the plains."

White Otter and the whites talked some more in sonorous, formal tones about welcome and friendship. After that the white men rode back into the settlement.

We continued at our slow pace, and camped on the banks of the Platte between the town and the mountains.

Crowds of curious whites gathered immediately, and stared at us as though they had never seen an Indian before, as though we were some sort of freaks. They talked among themselves and laughed and pointed. My face flushed with anger and shame, for their words were contemptuous and mocking, and they pointed at us in ridicule.

It is well, perhaps, that none other than myself in our village spoke or understood English. Otherwise there would undoubtedly have been trouble, with which we would have been ill prepared to cope. I contained my fury at their ridicule, and refused to translate their remarks to my Indian friends, though I was asked several times.

One woman pointed at me and shrilled, "Gracious, look at that scowling savage! He has blue eyes! Is he one of those 'breeds' I've heard so much talk about?"

I wanted to kill her, and the fat man with her, who was scolding her for making such an unladylike remark in public. I could hear some of his words: "Undoubtedly some of the white men out here consort with these dirty savages, but it's not something a lady talks about in public."

I discovered that I was trembling, that my fists were clenched until the nails bit into my palms. I stalked away, full of a murderous fury.

Our old men are fools! I told myself, but even as I thought it I knew it was not true. They were not fools, but simple, honorable men who were doing a thing they had solemnly considered, a thing they honestly believed to be right and good. They were heeding the words of Left Hand, chief of all the Southern Arapaho. They were going in friendship to the trespassers, the interlopers, in an attempt to build the foundation of a lasting peace.

But it was useless, as I had feared it would be. For the whites did not consider themselves interlopers, did not even consider the Indians individuals, fellow humans, who had rights and feelings the same as they. All that day the whites came to stare and point, to laugh and ridicule.

We erected our tepees, and when Red Stone's was up, I went into it and sat beside the fire. Pride forbade that we should broach the subject of trade for food immediately. We could not let them know we were destitute, hungry. So we sat beside our meatless fires and waited.

Yet even within Red Stone's tepee I could not escape the whites. They wandered into our lodges, uninvited, to poke at our possessions, to trample our beds, to ignore our privacy within our own homes. They even stole from us, carrying off as souvenirs many small articles that could be easily concealed within their garments.

The sun dropped behind the peaks to the west, and the whites at last drifted from our village. Now, with darkness over the land, they were afraid of us, believing us to be as they themselves were.

Indeed, night was a dangerous time in the infant city they called Denver. In the night, human predators lurked in the shadows and attacked others of their kind for the gold they carried upon their persons. Each shop and building must be locked, for if it were not, gangs of men would enter it while its occupants were away and steal its contents. Quarrels flared, too, in the night, as the white men filled their bellies with the fiery whisky that was sold to them in buildings built specially for that purpose. The sound of gunfire was frequent, as were the sounds of loud voices.

That night, because Red Stone looked so ill, I killed one of our dogs, and Beaver Woman cooked part of it over the fire. Before we ate, we burned a small piece of it as an offering to Ha-sananen.

I was amazed at the way Red Stone had wasted away. His skin had an unhealthy gray color. His cheeks were sunken, his eyes tired. When he coughed, which was often, the coughing racked his thin body and his face twisted with pain.

Yet his eyes, as always, were kind and wise. He said to me, "Patience, Sharp Knife. I can see your feelings upon your face. But you must not expect too much. The whites must learn to know us before they can like us. Give them the time they need to know us."

Time! Time! They would never know us because they did not want to.

Over the sounds of revelry and quarreling in the white men's town now arose a hail at the edge of our village. "Hey, you redskins! I'm comin' in. I got a barr'l o' rotgut whisky to trade."

I went out of the tepee and advanced toward the voice. I laid my hand on the handle of the Pawnee knife, then reluctantly took it away.

The men of our village, not knowing English, had not understood the man's words and did not follow. I said, "Take your damned rotgut back. We want food, not whisky. We'll trade, but only for food."

"Hey, Joe, one of 'em talks English. You a breed, son?"

I didn't answer, but I could feel my anger stir. The whiny voice said, "You ain't the chief. Reckon I'll just go in an' ask him does he want some whisky."

I felt a savage chuckle rise in my throat. I said, "Try it. I'll slit your throat from ear to ear."

"Whoa, now. Whoa, boy. We'll go back. Come on, Joe. Let's git the hell outa here."

I heard them stumbling away, leading a pack mule upon whose back was lashed a small oak barrel of whisky. I went back to the village.

I had sent these away, but I could not send them all away. I could not be on all sides of the village at once. When I got back to Red Stone's tepee, there was already a commotion at the far side of the village.

Four white men were there. One was like a bear, resembling Sonofabitch Smith. Another was tall and thin and hollow-cheeked. A third was wizened and small, with teeth that protruded like those of a prairie dog. The fourth was a young man, my age, a handsome man who wore a short gun at his waist. This one kept looking around hungrily, and I knew at once what was in his mind.

I said in English, "Go away. We do not want your whisky. We want to trade for food."

"Ain't got no food. Reckon you ain't talkin'

fer the others no way. They're hungry fer whisky right enough. Look at 'em."

I looked. Like dogs waiting for scraps they clustered around him. Behind me, Red Stone approached, coughing painfully. He joined the waiting braves.

I was beat, and knew it. I could not control the whole tribe.

I went to Red Stone's tepee and entered, angry and sick in my heart. I heard other white men come to the village, bearing the same trade goods, barrels of poor whisky.

The noise and confusion increased. Our men, under the influence of the liquor, whooped and screeched, forgetting momentarily the hunger that gnawed in their bellies, forgetting the despair and frustration that had dogged their heels so long.

They stripped their tepees of the few goods they had to trade, and Red Stone was one among them that did this. Nor did I have the desire to refuse him, for in the liquor he had forgotten his sickness. His cheeks were flushed for the first time in months, his eyes bright. He moved with a springy, youthful step, for all his staggering.

Besides, I knew his temper when he was drinking. Had I tried to stop him, I would have had to fight him, and that I could never do.

I remembered again those prophetic words, "They will lie with our squaws while we squat before our tepees and offer no protest," and Red Stone's "Never!"

Yet late in the night he staggered to our tepee, bringing the small white man with the protruding teeth, and called to Beaver Woman to come forth and be seen.

Pale but obedient, she would have gone, but I put a hand on her arm and said in a voice that made her eyes grow wide, "No. Go back to your bed. Red Stone is not himself or he would not do this."

I stepped from the flap of the lodge. The Pawnee knife was in my hand, a murderous fury within my heart. Red Stone caught at my arm, but I brushed him away.

Crouched like a panther, I moved on silent feet toward the white man, who began to drool from his loose-lipped mouth. His eyes grew wide like those of the rabbit when he faces the prairie wolf and cannot escape.

The white man saw death in my face. His protruding Adam's apple worked up and down as though he were a serpent trying to swallow a mouse. And then, with a choked cry, he whirled and ran.

I was not to be denied. The Pawnee knife would yet taste blood. All the outrage of the day and night was a fire within my heart.

I ran, and was near to overtaking him when I heard my name called in a voice that was more scream than shout. "Sharp Knife! Sharp Knife!"

It was the voice of Waanibe, Singing Wind. If there had been fury in my heart before, it was now doubled. If I had desired to kill, I was now obsessed with the need for it.

Forgotten was the small white man with the protruding teeth. Forgotten was all save Singing Wind, and her cry for help.

It seemed to take forever to reach the tepee of Gray Cloud. Yet it could not have been more than a few seconds. I burst through the entrance flap, stepping over the prone, snoring body of Gray Cloud as I did so.

Fury lashed me like lightning lashing out of a summer storm. Singing Wind was struggling with the young white man—the one who wore the short gun at his waist. On the floor at the far side of the tepee, Singing Wind's mother and another white man made a writhing blur upon the floor.

Behind me, Singing Wind's brother entered the tepee as I had entered, bursting through at a run. I supposed he had left the village earlier because the orgy sickened him. He glanced at me, then launched himself at the white man on the floor with his mother. His knife made a dull gleam in his hand.

It was all I saw of him, for my attention was now on the young white man. Perhaps he sensed his peril, for he released Singing Wind and his hand went like a shaft of light to the short gun at his waist. It bellowed, and fire leaped from its muzzle.

A leadenness, a complete lack of feeling invaded my left arm, but I felt no pain. In my right hand I held the Pawnee knife, sharp enough to shave the soft whiskers from my face. I struck him, and bore him backward, and drove the knife deep into his chest. When I withdrew it, a light froth bubbled from the hole it had made.

Again and again I plunged it into his body, until he moved no more, until the blood stopped flowing from his wounds. Then, seizing him by his long hair, I took his scalp and stuffed it into my belt.

Singing Wind said in a frightened voice, "It is done, Sharp Knife. I am proud, for you are very brave. But you are hurt, and the bodies of the white men must be hidden, else the others will say we have begun a war against them."

Sanity returned to me slowly. I did not regret what I had done. I would do it over, a thousand times if need be. But Singing Wind was wise and her words were true.

I let her put a poultice of ground mescal buttons upon my arm, which would heal quickly, for the bullet had passed cleanly through. She tied the poultice on with a strip of soft deerskin. Then Many Elks, her brother, and I dragged the bodies of the two white men from the tepee.

Had we been wise enough to forgo taking the white men's scalps, we would not have needed to worry, for death is commonplace among the whites at night. Yet their scalpless heads would instantly brand us their killers.

We dragged them for a great distance, until we were near to exhaustion. Then we covered the bodies with branches and leaves and grass, and piled stones upon these to hold them in place.

When we returned, Many Elks went to the tepee of White Otter, our chief, to confess what we had done, and to warn him that the white men might be missed, and the tribe blamed.

I went to Red Stone's tepee, for a runner had met me as I was returning to the village. He said that Red Stone was very ill, and near to death.

Gray was staining the eastern sky. The air was chill and damp, and a haze lay over the ground. There was the feel of snow in the air.

I heard Red Stone's tortured coughing as soon as I reached the tepee. The medicine men were there, mumbling over him, and one of them was extracting from his medicine bag a piece of a certain root called *niaata*, which is used for cough. The other was dripping an herbal concoction on the red coals of the fire, from which arose vaporous fumes.

Red Stone, sober now, but very sick, looked at me as I came in. He croaked, "My time has come and I will go to the place above. I must travel the land trails, as all who are not killed in battle must do. But before I go, my spirit will visit the friends I have known while I was here. Four days will I stay, and after that I will go."

I squatted down beside him, frightened and awed in the presence of death. I looked at the wasted form of Red Stone, and remembered him as he had once been, strong and proud and fleet of foot.

Only his eyes were the same, kind and wise as they looked into mine. He said, "Thank you, my son, for driving the white man from my tepee. I brought him only because my head was fogged with the medicine water. I am full of shame."

I said nothing. There seemed to be nothing to say. I had known Red Stone would regret what he had done last night, something he had never done before. What surprised me was that he remembered it at all.

He said, "Care for and protect Beaver Woman, for she has been as a mother to you. No mother could have loved you more than she, no father more than I."

I said, "Her tepee shall be filled with meat as long as I live. But enough of this talk. You are not going to die. You will live to lead me upon the warpath against our enemies. You will pierce the ears of my firstborn child."

Red Stone smiled. "No. There is fire in my lungs, blood in my breath when I cough."

Beaver Woman was weeping almost silently on the other side of him. He said, "Be strong and kind and wise. Heed the words of my friend Left Hand. But do not flinch from the things your heart tells you must be done."

I said, "My father is wise. I will heed his words." I meant to say the words strongly, but my voice caught in my throat and came out choked.

Red Stone's voice was weaker now. "You have chosen once between your Indian brothers and the whites. But you must choose many times. Consider your choice well each time, my son. Remember my words. There are good men and bad among the whites, just as there are among us. Revere the good you find in them, but do not condemn because there is also bad."

A chill coursed down my spine. Could it be that Red Stone was so close to Ha-sananen already that he echoed God's words to me?

His head fell back upon the ground. Beaver Woman's body shook with sobs she could not contain. My own throat was choked and I could not speak. Red Stone's eyes were fixed on me in death, the eyes of a father upon his son.

I put my head down into my hands and wept, not hearing the commotion outside the tepee, the noise and confusion as the village began to ready itself for moving.

Life cannot wait for death. The village moved, heading south again with bellies still empty. We buried Red Stone along the way, and shot his favorite horse so that it fell upon his grave.

Stirred up by the trader with the protruding teeth, who missed his two comrades and suspected their fate, the whites attacked the rear of our moving village, and the warriors of our band fell back and engaged them.

All day the battle raged, but in the late afternoon the whites drew away when a party of Cheyenne appeared against the horizon.

With the Cheyenne was Two Antelopes. And all that night he talked to the men of our village. At dawn the issue was decided. The treaty had been broken. We would drive the interlopers from our land.

Not today, or tomorrow, or even within a month. First the tribes must unite. Then we must have guns, for we could not win without them.

We would raid and withdraw, carrying what loot we had been able to seize. In time, we would all have guns and powder and balls. Then we would fall upon the whites and kill—kill until they fell back, until they retreated to the east where they belonged.

Once again the great plain would belong to the Arapaho, the Cheyenne, the Sioux. Once again the buffalo would roam upon it, countless as the grains of sand in the river bed.

There would be peace and plenty, and, for me, Singing Wind.

In time of hunger, dream of plenty. In time of peace, prepare for war. I was convinced at last that no other solution to the problem could be found.

Chapter Ten

A ND SO, hungry, poorly clothed, nearly destitute, we began our war against the whites who had invaded our land, who had broken the treaty they themselves had written in 1851.

We went into winter camp at the foot of the mountains some twenty-five miles south of Denver City. Because our people were desperate, the Cheyenne and Two Antelopes remained, and hunted in the foothills with us until we had killed enough deer, bear, and small game to keep the village eating while we were gone.

Then, riding our best horses, the young men of our village, myself included, rode eastward with Two Antelopes and the Cheyenne to attack and plunder the white caravans that even in winter still streamed across the plain. With us went the village's "dog soldiers," members of the men's age societies and fiercest of all Arapaho warriors, who in time of peace act as camp police-men to keep order and enforce the edicts of the chief.

I was filled with excitement, with the nervous-ness that untried warriors must ever experience before going into battle, be they Indian or white.

Would I have the courage that was needed? Would I be able to control my fear?

I thought of Singing Wind, and was reassured. For her I could do anything. I would take many white scalps and would return to her covered with glory.

Painted for war, dressed in our finest barbaric splendor, we rode from the village over fifty strong, while the squaws, the old men, and the warriors left behind as camp guards lined the path of our going and cheered us on with exhortations to be brave, unrelenting—to bring back much loot from the white caravans, many white scalps to give us honor within the tribe.

I carried the scalp of the young white man aloft at the tip of my lance proudly, my white blood forgotten now. For in this was the glory that all young men experience as they march away to war.

I passed Singing Wind, and her heart was in her eyes as she looked upon me. But she also smiled at Two Antelopes and waved to him, remembering, perhaps, that in the old days we had been three.

Then we were clear of the village, hearing the cries raised behind us and proud as we had never been proud before.

Two Antelopes looked at me. He looked at the white man's scalp that I carried aloft on my lance. His glance was inscrutable. He had always kept his feelings hidden, even when we were boys and close to each other. But I had grown to know him well. When his face was closed, as it was now, it meant he was filled with hate and jealousy and sour bad temper.

His words revealed none of this, however. He said, "You have done well in my absence. Does the Pawnee knife like the taste of white blood?"

I tried to summon the warmth I had once felt for him, and believe I succeeded fairly well. I grinned at him and he grinned back. On the surface, at least, things were once again the same as they had been between us so long ago.

Two Antelopes had changed during his absence. He had grown tall, and though he was still thin, his muscles were like the sinews of the buffalo. He had learned to smile with his mouth, but his eyes were still brooding, still cold. He had traveled far with the Cheyenne, to the new stone fort that William Bent had built at Big Timbers. He had been south among the Comanches and Kiowas, and told chilling tales of their cruelty to captured prisoners.

Cruelty to prisoners was not the way of the Arapaho. We were taught to treat them with consideration. If an enemy must be killed, kill him. But do it quickly. In later years there were instances of torture by Arapaho and Cheyenne, but that was after Sand Creek, after the white man had so savagely earned our bitterest hatred.

The change in Two Antelopes was more than one of appearance. He had changed inside as well. When he told the tales of Kiowa and Comanche cruelties, his eyes glowed, as though even thinking of the torture gave him a sharp kind of pleasure. I felt an uneasiness that for the moment cooled my joy in being with him again.

Onward we rode throughout the day and at noon it began to snow. We were not so warmly dressed as we should have been, and many of us suffered from the cold.

That night we were fortunate enough to kill an old buffalo cow, and so were not forced to draw upon the small amount of pemmican we carried with us.

In the morning it was still snowing. The temperature had fallen during the night to a bitter level. We all began to think of our warm lodges at home.

Go back? Though many of us longed to go back, none would suggest it. We had come to drive the invaders from our land, to plunder their caravans. We had promised the village much loot, many guns, many scalps. We could not go back without them. And so we went on.

Because we were cold and had lost heart, we attacked without adequate preparation or scouting. What appeared to be an ordinary caravan of immigrants turned out to be a powerful, well-armed one.

We swept down upon them out of the snow-storm, taking them completely by surprise. They should never have recovered from their surprise, but they did. Fantastically, they recovered immediately, and the huge wagons lumbered into a circle from behind which poured the murderous fire of their breech-loading carbines.

Black Dog the Cheyenne fell, and Walking Horse, and Broken Pipe. We drew away, our charge broken. We went in again, and this time Old Hawk and White Sand fell. Walks-at-Night was wounded, and fell from his horse. He scrambled to his feet and tried to charge the embattled caravan afoot, but his wounded leg would not support him and he fell again. I was surprised to find myself riding full tilt toward him, hanging from the neck of my horse. Somehow I got him to the back of my horse, and together we rode out of range without being hit.

In numbers we had not been seriously hurt. But our spirit was utterly crushed by this ignominious defeat, and we had no desire to continue the attack. We fell back and waited, and when the caravan had gone on, we retrieved the bodies of our dead.

Many among us were for going back, for giving up the war until spring should come, and spring's warm days and nights. Two Antelopes mocked these fainthearted ones bitterly and sent them away with Walks-at-Night and the bodies of the dead.

Now we numbered but twenty warriors, yet among these were all the "dog soldiers" of the village, and most of the Cheyenne who had been with Two Antelopes.

We went into camp beneath a bluff until the storm should clear, and when it did we were rested and well fed and strong again.

The second caravan we scouted for two whole days, until we knew its habits, its weakness, its strength.

They were a late-rising lot, for one thing. Often their camp did not come to life until the sky was beginning to turn pink with sunrise. And it was a small caravan, of but five wagons.

At dawn of the third day we left our horses and crept up on them.

The fire in the center of their camp circle had burned down to ashes. A single man sat dozing beside it. The others slept soundly, judging from the snores coming from the wagons.

By prearranged agreement, we crept into the camp. Two Antelopes was to kill the guard by the fire. The rest of us were to enter the wagons, one from each end, while the remainder of our party waited to take care of any unexpected resistance that might develop.

It was a cold, clear morning. Vapor blew from our mouths and nostrils in great clouds. The snow squeaked lightly under our stealthy moccasins.

A great excitement grew in my body. My muscles were tense, and I discovered that I was trembling violently, as though from cold. My hand clutched the Pawnee knife tightly as I crept to the forward end of the wagon I was to attack. Night Horse the Cheyenne approached the rear.

Suddenly a shout came from the guard beside the fire, a shout that instantly changed to a gurgling gasp as Two Antelopes' knife sank into his body.

At once there was a flurry of motion within the wagon assigned to me. I leaped on the seat, and my glance swept the interior as I flung aside the canvas flap.

A bearded white man was sitting up, trying to throw off his blankets. His graying hair was tousled, and his eyes were wide with surprise and dazed with his sudden awakening. His hand flashed toward the holstered short gun that hung from a peg beside him. I knew I could not reach him with the knife before he reached the gun. I drew back my hand to throw it.

But at that instant, Night Horse leaped upon him, knife flashing as he buried it in the white man's back.

The fight, if fight it could be called, was over almost before it had begun. We dragged the bodies of the dead whites, all men, from their wagons, and those who had killed them took their scalps. Others among us touched their bodies, counting coups as is allowed by Arapaho custom. Four warriors may count coup upon a dead enemy simply by touching his body with a weapon held in the hand, tomahawk, bow, knife, or gun.

After that we turned to the wagons. We took from them bolts of cloth for the women of the village, guns, powder, and balls for ourselves. We gorged ourselves upon the provisions we could not take, and loaded what we could on our horses' backs in cloth sacks tied together so that one hung on each side of the horse. We found a wooden box, which puzzled my comrades, but which I opened, remembering boxes from my childhood. It contained hard candy, which I also remembered, but which I had not seen these many years. After their first cautious taste, the warriors were like children, and buried their hands deep in the box of candy, afterward stuffing it into their mouths until I thought some of them would choke.

Perhaps it was the candy, and the memories its taste brought back to me. But suddenly I looked at the bodies of the white men on the ground, their heads like the skinned carcasses of animals, and felt a stir of pity and guilt.

The old pattern was being repeated. We had been wronged by a few white traders in Denver City, so we turned our vengeance upon these wholly innocent men, freshly arrived from the East, who had no connection at all with those who had wronged us, who probably did not even know they were invading our land in direct violation of a treaty.

It occurred to me that my father's body must have looked much like one of these after the attack in which I was captured.

Suddenly I had no taste for more of this, and wanted only to be back at the village, where all things were familiar, where right and wrong were clear-cut and therefore easily understood.

I know something else now that I did not realize then. In some deep recess of my mind, I feared the time when we would fall upon a caravan with which women were traveling. I feared it because I did not know what I would do when it happened. For in that same deep recess of my mind was the memory of my mother's awful screams as the young warriors carried her away.

Would I turn on my friends when I heard screams issuing from the lips of yet another white woman? Would the terror of that day come back so strongly as to rob me of reason and control? Would white blood or Indian training triumph? Because I didn't know, I feared the thing that would force my final, irrevocable decision. Fortunately for me, those two raids were the beginning and end of our war with the whites for that year, at least.

Returning to our village, we met a party of older warriors accompanying Chief Left Hand of the Arapaho and Chief Black Kettle of the Cheyenne. Both were in a towering rage, having met the defeated of our party who had returned earlier to our village. "Who do you think you are?" raged Left Hand. "Where did you get the authority to declare and wage war upon the white when the policy of both our tribes is to stay at peace?"

Even now, he said, a treaty was being written by the head chief of the Long Knives in Washington, and this new treaty would not be broken. It would give the whites that which they had already taken and no more. What remained would belong to the Arapaho, the Cheyenne, the Sioux.

Two Antelopes sneered, "For how long, Left Hand? For how long will the remainder be inviolate?"

I thought Left Hand would strike him. He controlled himself with obvious difficulty.

Left Hand had matured greatly since I had last seen him. Not yet thirty-five, he had been chief of all the Southern Arapaho for several years. The responsibility had taken its toll of him. Lines of sadness and worry traced his face. His eyes were weary.

His was a monumental task. I could see that even then. Knowing in his heart that a way to peace must be found if the Indian were to survive, he was met by obstacles at every turn.

He wanted his people to become farmers, as they once had been long ago, before the white men set foot on the American Continent. But the old skills, the old knowledge were gone. Not even the oldest members of the tribe could remember the time when we planted and reaped from the ground, although these things were part of our folklore.

So, through William Bent, Left Hand implored the government to provide the Arapaho and Cheyenne with farm implements, with seed, with men who would instruct them in the ways of tilling the land.

They ignored his request, clinging to the old beliefs that Indians would not work, that they did not really want to farm. Besides, it was easier and cheaper to continue providing trade blankets, food, ammunition, and trinkets—easier to pacify the Indians and postpone the inevitable than to seek a permanent solution of the conflict.

Within the tribe, Left Hand faced similar short-sightedness and resistance to his suggestions. The young men were growing restive and resentful. More and more like Two Antelopes raised their voices demanding obliteration of the whites, demanding war to the finish.

Chastened and subdued, our glory stolen, we returned to the village, and our welcome was dampened by the disapproving presence of Left

Hand and Black Kettle, both of whom wanted the stolen articles returned, but at the same time feared their return because it would bring the white men's wrath down upon our village.

Much of the loot I had taken I put upon the pile in the center of the village to be distributed among the people. I gave a long length of red silk to Beaver Woman, and it brought a smile to her haggard face for the first time since the death of Red Stone. She had amputated both her little fingers at the first joint as a sign of grief for Red Stone, and had cut her braids as well. Her face was pale, and her eyes were dull and without luster.

I embraced her and kissed her cheek. My throat felt tight, so I drew away and playfully draped the red silk about her shoulders. "You are as pretty as a maiden."

There were bright tears in her dark eyes. She said, "Do not linger here with this old woman. Have you no gifts for Singing Wind?"

Indeed I had. I had part of a bolt of bright-flowered calico that would make Singing Wind beautiful as the prairie flowers in early spring. I had a necklace of shiny red beads I had found in a small wooden box in one of the looted wagons. Altogether I had returned with more things than the trader Sonofabitch Smith had brought to our village in all the trips he had made to it.

I went from our tepee to that of Singing Wind.

Gray Cloud was squatted before his tepee. I laid down a small sack of food at his feet and said, "It is yours, Gray Cloud."

Looking up, I could see Singing Wind peeping at me from the entrance flap of the tepee. I laid her gifts down beside the sack. I said, "These are also yours, but they are woman's things, for which you will have no use. Perhaps Singing Wind can use them."

Then I went away, but my eyes promised Singing Wind that I would return as soon as it was dark.

When I got back to Beaver Woman's tepee, Left Hand was waiting for me. "I grieve for you, Sharp Knife. I grieve with you for Red Stone, for I have just heard of his death."

I got out Red Stone's pipe and packed it. I took a twig from the fire and lighted it. I pointed the stem at the heavens, the earth, and at the four cardinal directions. I was a man now, and this was my lodge.

I said, "Your presence honors us," smoked, and then handed Left Hand the pipe.

He smoked for a moment, then said, "Already the white men outnumber us, as Ha-sananen told me they would. And still they come. But there is some hope for us, because even now the whites quarrel among themselves over the question of whether white men have the right to own black men as slaves. If we wait and be patient, perhaps the white men will kill each other until there are no more left. Then the land will again belong to us."

I said, "You are very wise, and I have been a child. I have let my anger make me thoughtless. The earth is my father, the sky my mother. And Left Hand is my chief. I will not be foolish and thoughtless again."

He smiled at me and rose. "The Arapaho will wait. It is the only way."

He rode out of the village with Black Kettle and the warriors that accompanied them.

When night came I went to Gray Cloud's lodge and changed the setting of the smoke flap, smiling to myself because it must be obvious to Gray Cloud by now that the wind did not change so often. But his voice held the same tone it always had as he said, "The wind has changed, Waanibe. Go out and fix the smoke flap."

She came out to me, into my arms at once, soft and fragrant as a dove. She kissed me upon the lips, then drew back and said in a breathless, worried voice, "Two Antelopes has given my brother five horses and has asked for me as his wife."

"And what has Many Elks answered?" I felt as though the pit of my stomach were gone. My legs were like water.

"Many Elks says Two Antelopes is *haha-ka* as Eagle Feather was. He also says that Two

Antelopes is too young to take a squaw. He asked me if I wished to become the bride of Two Antelopes. I told him no. So he will return the horses."

Relief drained what strength remained in me. Singing Wind's hand tightened on my arm. "Two Antelopes will know why the horses were returned. The whole village will know. So Two Antelopes will seek you out and try to kill you. He is the son of Eagle Feather, and *haha-ka* enough to attack you from behind. Be careful, Sharp Knife. My heart will die if you die."

Inside the tepee, Gray Cloud began to cough. Singing Wind ran to change the smoke flap, which she and I both had forgotten. When she had finished, she said breathlessly, "I must go in. Wait for me beside the stream when I go for water in the morning."

She touched her lips to my cheek and was gone.

I stood for a moment, staring at Gray Cloud's lodge. Somewhere in the village I could hear the weird, nigh indescribable chorus of a gaming song, rising, falling, stopping, starting. It was a sound I had not heard for a long time. Indeed, it had been a long time since our men had anything with which to gamble.

They played with the *ga-qaa*, a button that was passed from hand to hand among the members of one side while the members of the other side tried to guess who held it, and in which hand.

Perhaps it was the noise that made me miss the slight sound behind me. Perhaps it was my own intent thoughts. But miss it I did, and missing it almost cost me my life.

My ears caught a second sound, like a sigh, and this was the sound of the garments upon a swiftly moving man.

Instantly my mind cried, Two Antelopes! Instinct and training made me fling myself violently to one side while my hand automatically grasped the handle of the Pawnee knife at my waist.

He brushed against me, throwing me further off balance, and I sprawled to the ground, my fringed shirt slashed from shoulder to waist and my hide beneath it similarly slashed.

Blood wet my back instantly, warm and sticky. I rolled and brought my feet under me like a cat. Crouching, I faced him, tense as a coiled rattlesnake, my hands held away from my body to give me balance and the power to strike instantly.

He was a silent shadow, enraged and disappointed because he had failed to kill with his first rush.

Noiseless save for our harsh, tight breathing, we circled much as two sparring buffalo bulls will circle before they charge. I doubt if even Gray Cloud and Singing Wind, inside the tepee before which we fought, heard us.

He whispered, "Eagle Feather, my father, has

returned. Upon you will he do the penance of the murderer. Upon you, with the whole village and Singing Wind as witnesses."

He was indeed crazy, more crazy than Eagle Feather had ever been. Gone was the Two Antelopes I had known, gone the one who had been my friend. Gone was his determination to kill his father and avenge his mother. Now he was allied with Eagle Feather, condoning his father's crime, committing one himself so that his father might earn back his place in the tribe.

He did not even realize that the tribe would refuse to accept the penance, worked upon me, a member of the tribe. But he probably considered me now, as he no doubt always had deep within him, a white, an enemy, and not a member of the tribe at all.

I heard my own voice saying, "You'll have to kill me first, eater of flesh, and that you can never do."

The taunt brought him in with a rush. I leaped aside, twisting my body, and his knife slashed the air viciously an inch from my belly. As he went past, I drove the Pawnee knife at him, felt it bite into his shoulder, and heard his sharply indrawn breath.

The knife could not have slashed him deeply, for he whirled, seemingly unhurt, snarling deep within his throat.

My own wound was bleeding freely. Already

my breechclout and leggings were soaked with blood. My leggings were stuck to my thighs with it, and I could feel weakness from the wound coming over me like a cloud. This must be ended, and quickly, else he would kill me as he promised.

Taunt him into another charge, I thought. And this time be swift in evading it, swift in striking the death blow.

I sneered, "You are more *haha-ka* than Eagle Feather ever was, but you and he are two of a kind. Eagle Feather murders squaws, and you strike from behind because you fear to attack from the front."

The taunt achieved the desired result. I had not finished speaking before Two Antelopes launched his charge.

So swift was he, so deadly quick, that I was again caught off guard in spite of my determination not to be. There was no time to dodge, no time for anything but a frantic grab at his knife wrist with my left hand, a wordless, unspoken prayer to Ha-sananen.

My hand slipped upon his bloody wrist, grabbed again, closed upon it a second time. It was like holding a serpent.

Now his left hand found my knife wrist, and all the time we were straining, pushing at one another, trying to break free.

The sharp, friendly smell of wood smoke and

cooking meat drifted into my nostrils. To my ears came the sounds of the village, the gaming song, a laughing child, a warrior quarreling with his squaw, the querulous voice of an old man, a barking dog. These were the sounds of life—a good life—which I would leave in an instant if I failed to strike Two Antelopes down.

I could feel new strength flowing into my body. The Pawnee knife drove forward savagely as I tore free from his clutching left hand upon my wrist. I felt it strike a rib, slide off, felt it sink to the hilt in his body.

Instantly withdrawing it, I leaped back. As I did so I released my precarious hold on his knife wrist an instant too soon and felt the burn of his sharp blade along my forearm.

But I was clear; bleeding and weakening, but clear.

Around me there were now light and life. Members of the band, hearing the noise of our fighting, had come from their tepees, carrying torches of firewood.

A pair of "dog soldiers" seized me, but there was no need for them to seize Two Antelopes. He was bent almost double, clutching his belly. He looked at me, blood on his lips, and croaked, "May you wander forever between the earth and the sky. May you never find the peace that all men seek."

His face twisted with a spasm of pain. Still

clutching his belly, he folded quietly into the dust.

Now, at once everyone began to talk excitedly. White Otter, the chief, arrived at a run. "How did the fight start?" he demanded.

"Two Antelopes attacked me from behind." I turned and displayed my bloodsoaked back.

My weakness was returning. My head whirled, and no longer could I see White Otter clearly. But my mind would not release its memory of Two Antelopes' dying curse: "May you wander forever between the earth and the sky. May you never find the peace that all men seek."

A chill stole over my body, for in me, as in all Arapaho, was a fear of curses and witching. True, Two Antelopes was not a medicine man, and therefore he was probably unable, while he lived, to issue an effective curse. Yet who could say whether the curse was uttered while he still lived, or whether it was uttered by his spirit, after death?

I felt my knees turn to water. I felt the strength leave my body. The Pawnee knife slipped from my hand, and but for the grasp of the two "dog soldiers," I would have fallen. Then, while my head whirled crazily, I felt other hands upon me, and I was being carried through the village.

A soft voice was in my ear, a voice filled with worry, with terror that I would die, with love and tenderness. "Courage, Sharp Knife. You will not die. You will yet live to give me many sons, to kill many buffalo, to follow many paths of war."

Then familiar things were around me, familiar smells, and I knew I was in the tepee of Beaver Woman.

I felt nothing as Singing Wind stanched the flow of my wounds with clean earth. I was in a world of darkness that was like death.

Chapter Eleven

MY RETURN TO LIFE was slow, like the changing of the seasons. I had lost much blood, and recovered slowly.

For days I lay unconscious, and when I did regain my senses, it was for but short periods at a time. Always, it seemed, Singing Wind was near, as was Beaver Woman. My illness must have dimmed her grief, for when I was able to notice things again, I saw that color had returned to her cheeks and life to her eyes.

The winter passed while I lay weak, and helpless, wasted away until I was but skin and bones. Sometimes it seemed that I was again a boy, newly captured and adopted, for Beaver Woman came to me very often during both day and night and made me eat. If I refused, she would spoon broth or tender bits of meat into my mouth until I was forced to chew and swallow.

Spring came, and returning strength to me. Now I sat often in the sun outside the tepee and watched the children playing, watched the men ride out to the hunt and return.

Often they came in empty-handed. Yet they killed enough game to supply a bare existence for the village, though everyone was unusually thin. And never did they fail to leave meat at our tepee, knowing that now there was no one in it able to hunt.

In late spring I began to walk near the village, and to ride horseback again. After that, my body gained weight swiftly, so that soon I was able to join the hunts.

Two Antelopes was dead, yet his curse remained in my mind. My weakness had made it seem stronger, more dangerous than it really was. Telling myself to disregard the curse had no effect. It troubled and worried me, perhaps because in my own mind I knew I was doomed to be forever neither red nor white, to wander, as Two Antelopes had directed, between the earth and the sky.

The treaty Left Hand had mentioned was supposed to have been signed in the fall, but was not, since the tribes failed to assemble. Too busy were they, hunting for the winter, desperately hunting, since game for their daily needs was hard enough to find, let alone game to dry and store for winter use.

I continued to see Singing Wind, continued to fight in my mind against the custom that forbids the marriage of a young warrior in his early twenties.

The winter came, and we hunted continually, sometimes not returning to the village for days at a time. The people were hungry, and the children cried for food. So when a runner came from the new Indian agent, Boone, at Big Timbers, saying the treaty was ready for signing, that gifts and food were there for the Indians, we packed up our village and started south, beggars who must accept the white man's charity to keep the bellies of their children filled.

It was February, by the white man's reckoning of time, and bitterly cold. Our buffalo robes were worn and thin. Our moccasins were old and without warmth. Small wonder we were angry when, on arriving, we found that the treaty had already been signed, the gifts already distributed.

Boone had arbitrarily selected six chiefs to sit in council with him, when he should have allowed the tribes to send him their main chiefs. In his ignorance, he had acted hastily, before all the bands were gathered. The result was only to be expected. Most of both tribes, Cheyenne and Arapaho, refused to accept the terms of the treaty that had been negotiated and signed without their knowledge or consent. Their resentment was increased by the fact that they had traveled far for food and clothing, only to find it already gone.

They stayed on hopefully, resentfully, at Big Timbers, about which had been built a Long Knife encampment called Fort Wise, but when it became apparent that there were to be no gifts, when their food began to run low, they sullenly packed up and departed.

The treaty that Left Hand had hailed as our salvation turned out to be a hollow mockery, a worthless promise by the white men to hold the remainder of our land inviolate, while even as it was signed, more whites poured along the Smoky Hill trail, and along a new trail to the north that followed the Platte.

In the spring, stagecoaches ran along still more new roads with the wagons and men on horseback. Also in the spring came news that the white men were fighting each other over a place called Fort Sumter.

Hope again for the Indians. Hope that died because the flood of immigrants did not slow and stop. The white man's war seemed to have no effect on the unending hordes that invaded our land.

They shot the buffalo for sport from the windows of their stagecoaches. They built more towns and they made more roads. Their volunteer troops marched back and forth across the prairie for practice. They ran the wild game just for fun, and fired warning shots at parties of Indians that approached curiously to watch.

Each village divided. Each had its war faction of young men who scoffed at the restraint of the old ones, who demanded retaliation before it would be too late. And each had its cooler heads, who preached the words of Left Hand and demanded that the young ones obey.

Men from the Confederacy approached our chiefs, offering many gifts if we would join them in their war against the North. Uncertain, our chiefs went to Big Timbers and asked William Bent, the trusted friend of the Cheyenne, for advice. Bent told them to wait, to stay out of the white men's quarrels. And so they did.

Yet the inevitable friction between two races who neither understood each other nor wanted to continued. News trickled into our village of incident after incident. A hunting party crossed a road unexpectedly at the same time a coach was passing. Nervous whites fired from the windows of the coach. An Indian was wounded. There followed a chase by the outraged Indians. The result? A burned coach, butchered horses, dead white men, kidnaped women.

New indignation in Denver City, new indignation among the Indians. More distrust, more nervous trigger fingers. Worst of all was the feeling within my own village. Friends who had accepted me as wholly Arapaho for most of my life now looked upon me with wondering in their eyes, and I knew their thoughts. Would I remain with the Arapaho, faithful to them? Would I fight with them when the time for fighting came?

In my mind I almost welcomed the thought of conflict with the whites. Let it come, I thought, and I will show the Arapaho where Sharp Knife stands.

It came to our village, unexpectedly and terribly. And when it was over, not even Left Hand could have held us in check.

We were camped on Bijou Creek, east of the town of Denver. Several young warriors of the village had just returned from a raid on a Pawnee village with about twenty captured horses. There was much jubilation within the village, not only because of the horses, but also because a hunting party, of which I was a member, had just returned loaded with buffalo meat. There would be feasting, and dancing to the beat of the drum, and for a while, at least, we would convince ourselves that the good days had returned, that things were as they once had been.

As the sun sank behind the distant mountains, the bellies of the half-naked children were distended with the sudden plentiful supply of meat. And all were happy, smiling, and calling out to each other.

And then the *ga-ahine-na* called, "The Long Knives approach. A large party."

Immediately White Otter called for a group to go out and meet them. I went along as interpreter, since it was not known whether the Long Knives would have one with them.

By the time we caught our horses and rode from the village, they had approached to within a mile of it. Seeing us, they halted, and spread out in a long line facing us. I judged there were twenty or more, blue-clad cavalrymen wearing the wide-brimmed hats that were part of their uniform.

Touching my left breast with my right hand, I said in English, "Welcome to the village of White Otter."

Their leader wore the bar of a lieutenant. He was a short man, and fat, with long flowing mustaches and cold gray eyes. He said, "Hell! I didn't expect a redskin that talked English." He hesitated a moment, not smiling, just looking me over from head to foot. Anger stirred within me, so contemptuous was his appraisal. At last he said, "A breed, huh? An English-talkin' breed."

I said, "I am Sharp Knife, and I am an Arapaho. You are welcome to our village, but why do you come? We live at peace with the Long Knives."

He snorted, "Peace! The hell you do, you thievin' bastards! Ain't a white man in the territory that hasn't lost horses. I'm here to look over your herd. I'm here to take back any that wears a white man's brand."

I know my face turned white with anger. I could feel the scrutiny of my comrades, so I turned and translated. Then I sent a young man back to tell White Otter what the whites wanted and receive his instructions. I turned back to the lieutenant. "I have sent someone to talk to White Otter, our chief, and to ask for instructions. Please wait until he returns."

"Wait, hell! I got other things to do. We'll just ride through your horse herd and take a look."

I shrugged. I was not prepared to try to stop him, since I knew White Otter would want no trouble. I said, "We have nothing to hide. We have not stolen from the whites."

The lieutenant shouted an order, and his detachment wheeled toward our horse herd. I called out to the horse guards not to interfere.

Our small party, numbering less than ten, rode along behind the cavalrymen, who kept looking uneasily over their shoulders as though they expected us to attack.

The lieutenant picked two of his men and ordered them to ride through the horse herd while the remainder surrounded it to hold it in place. These two kept calling out to him, calling out brands that they read on the horses' hips.

I felt a sinking within my stomach. The Pawnee horses, the ones that had only that day been brought to the village and put with the herd. The Pawnees had no doubt stolen some of them from the whites.

But would the lieutenant believe that? Would he believe we were without guilt? I knew he wouldn't.

Quickly I turned to Walks-at-Night, who sat his horse close beside me. "The Long Knives have found the horses they seek among those taken from the Pawnees. There will be trouble. Ride swiftly to the village and warn them to get ready."

Walks-at-Night whirled his horse away and drummed with his heels upon its sides. He had gone no more than twenty yards when I heard the lieutenant issue a crisp order: "Get that one, goddamn it! Get him before he can reach the village!"

Half a dozen carbines barked, a ragged, staccato volley that I knew would do that which I had instructed Walks-at-Night to do. The village would be alerted, and ready for the attack.

Walks-at-Night's horse seemed to stumble. His head went down, and he fell heavily upon his back. Walks-at-Night was thrown clear, but he struck the ground with his body wholly limp and did not move afterward.

Before the echo of the volley died away, I was shouting, "Take cover! We must hold them here until the men from the village arrive!"

Unexpectedly, the horse herd gave us the time we needed. The sharp sounds of the rifles drove them into a frenzy. They milled wildly for an instant, then broke, running, straight through the ranks of the troopers.

Half a dozen of the whites were carried along with them. The others rallied around the now bellowing lieutenant, but it was several moments before they had recovered sufficiently to begin firing at us. By that time we were down on our bellies in a shallow ravine.

A few among us had guns, and I was one of these. The rest had only their bows and arrows. Yet the combination of bows and arrows and guns worked well in combat. Arrows, fired from the concealment of the ravine, kept the troopers' heads down so that those of us with rifles were able to fire without undue fear of showing ourselves.

A trooper howled, and afterward groaned almost continuously. Another rose to his feet and tried to run away, but fell with an arrow in his back.

The lieutenant's voice shouted, "Hey, you, the breed! Mebbe we made a mistake."

I smiled grimly to myself, and raised my own voice. "You made a mistake, all right. It was in shooting Walks-at-Night. Now you will die, and your men with you."

There was no more exchange of words. Only bullets. Behind us, the other men of the village came up, and entered the ravine. Afterward they joined their fire with ours.

Another trooper died, and another. But the light was fading. Soon it would be too dark to shoot. The white men would get away in the darkness.

I had forgotten the half-dozen troopers who had been carried away with the horses when they stampeded. But a sudden volley of shots back within the village brought them instantly to my mind.

Immediately we scrambled to our feet. Those of us who could, caught our horses. The others ran toward the village afoot, while the whites behind poured heavy fire into their ranks. Because of the darkness their aim was bad, and we had already forgotten them. In our hearts was fear for the women and children of the village, fear for the old ones, who were helpless and without weapons.

My heels beat a terrible, swift tattoo on the ribs of my horse. My heart was sick with fear— fear for Beaver Woman, for Singing Wind. I was ashamed because I had not anticipated this.

No doubt the six had soon broken free of the stampeding horses. Returning, they had heard the firing, had known their comrades would be overwhelmed. So they had circled to create a diversion by attacking the village behind us.

When we arrived at the village, the white men had gone. Theirs had been merely a hit-and-run action, designed to draw us back to protect our village.

Three small children lay dead near the tepee of the sacred pipe. A squaw, White Otter's youngest wife, lay where she had fallen trying to reach them, to cover them with her own body.

This was all, but it was enough. Equipping

ourselves swiftly, we set out to overtake the white men, to wipe them out.

We were too late. Our horses were badly scattered, and too much time was lost in rounding them up. By the time we were ready, the whites had a two-hour start.

Nor could we track them this night, for not even a star was showing. Clouds filled the sky, and it was so black a man could scarcely see the head of his horse before him.

Knowing they had a start on us, knowing they would escape and that they would immediately bring more of their kind down upon us, we had no choice but to flee. So we spent the remainder of the night packing up our belongings and getting ready to travel.

Luckily for us, a heavy rain began late in the afternoon of the following day, and wiped out the tracks of our moving village. But we did not stop until we had put a hundred miles between ourselves and the camp on Bijou Creek, until we reached another, larger village with which we could merge and be lost.

We had done no wrong. Yet Walks-at-Night had been killed. White Otter's young squaw had been killed. Three helpless children had been killed.

White Otter called the men into council. Left Hand was a woman, he said. If the whites wanted war, let them have war.

There were no dissenting voices among us. We would go to war, for a second time. Only this time Left Hand would not dissuade us. This time the whites would pay for their wrongs.

Chapter Twelve

FOR THREE TERRIBLE WEEKS we rode, plundering and killing, burning and destroying. No wagon train was safe, no stagecoach, no outlying farm or ranch. Yet our operations were necessarily limited to small wagon trains and poorly armed coaches, for our numbers were small because of the previous deaths among us.

We added twenty or thirty rifles to our arsenal, several kegs of powder, hundreds of pounds of lead for molding bullets. We captured blankets and clothing and dozens of small items that took our fancy.

We separated again from the large village we had previously joined, for they did not want us with them, fearing both the wrath of Left Hand and the wrath of the whites.

Among us, none rode harder than Sharp Knife, none was fiercer or more unrelenting. Three new scalps adorned my belt. New respect shone from the eyes of my comrades when they looked at me. I was proving myself. Soon none would dare point at me and say, "He is of the enemy and will turn against us."

The days grew cooler, the night air sharper with the approach of fall.

And there came a day, as inevitably it had to come, when we rode howling down a swiftly traveling stagecoach and heard the shrill cry of a woman from within.

Riding like screaming demons, we overtook the coach. The tone of my comrades' yells had changed to one of lusting anticipation. Within my heart, for the first time, was dark, cold fear. The time of decision was here, the time to find out whether Sharp Knife was truly Arapaho, or whether he was still a white.

The driver of the coach tumbled from the box with an arrow in his throat. The reins fell from his hands and dragged along the ground beneath the coach. A man leaned from the coach window and began firing at us. I rode close, raised my rifle, and fired its single bullet into his chest.

We had a pattern to follow in stagecoach attacks. First we eliminated all resistance by killing everyone who could fire a gun. Then we would shoot one of the horses. The horse would fall, hopelessly entangling the others and bringing the coach to a crashing halt. After that it was easy to pull the passengers that remained from the coach wreckage and kill them.

The pattern was no different today. One of the lead horses went down, an arrow in his neck. Immediately the others piled up on him, thrashing, with almost human screams of terror issuing from their throats. The coach piled into the down horses, lurched violently, and then whipped around and fell onto its side in a tremendous cloud of dust.

Again I heard the white woman scream, a lost, awful sound that struck chills to my heart. I began to hope that she would be killed in the crash, for then I would not have to face what I knew was coming.

Red Willow sprang from his horse and in running leaps made for the coach. Knife in hand, he leaped inside.

Running, I could not halt the image that sprang into my mind. It was an image of a woman and a small boy in an overturned carriage. I saw Red Stone again in my mind, a tortoise-shell comb stuck in his greasy hair. I heard my mother's terrible screaming.

I believe right then I went a little crazy myself. The Pawnee knife was in my hand and I reached the coach just as Red Willow climbed from it with the struggling, screaming form of a woman in his grasp. He was laughing. She had smeared his red war paint over his face while scratching it, and his blood mingled with the red paint on her hands.

I drew back my arm to drive the Pawnee knife into his body, but suddenly I stopped. What was I doing? This was Red Willow, my friend. I was Sharp Knife, an Indian. What did I care for the white woman?

I turned my glance deliberately away from her, from the lusting face of Red Willow, but not before I had seen her.

She was young, slim as Singing Wind. Her skin was pale, as translucent as the petals of a sand lily. Her eyes were the color of mine, blue. Her clothing was voluminous, containing enough yards of cloth to make dresses for half a dozen Indian women. But in her struggling with Red Willow it had been partly torn away from her body, revealing a white throat in which an incredibly fast pulse beat, and the rounded swell of her breasts beneath.

She continued to scream until I thought the sounds would drive me insane. They beat upon my eardrums and went beyond, echoing through my mind until I thought I could no longer endure it.

Red Willow carried the struggling white woman toward his horse. Her hair had come undone and streamed out in a red-gold cascade that reached nearly to her waist. He was laughing exultantly. "We have a young one, my comrades, a beautiful one, one with much life in her body!"

The others chuckled, made a few lewd remarks, and went on with their task of looting the coach.

I stood very still, grasping the spoke of a coach wheel with my hands so tightly that the knuckles were white.

The looting, in which I took no part, was soon

finished. Still I stood, gripping the spoke of the wheel, fighting my battle within myself. They noticed my strangeness, and Many Elks, the brother of Singing Wind, touched my shoulder and said, "Sharp Knife is troubled. His face is filled with strain and his eyes stare oddly."

I forced myself to speak between clenched teeth. "It is my hatred for the whites. It has overcome me until I am not myself."

This was something an Arapaho could understand, something he could admire—hatred so great as to defy comparison, hatred that consumed, that overwhelmed. He gripped my shoulder in approval.

The looting done, we set fire to the coach with coals one of us carried smoldering within a hollowed buffalo horn. We cut the throats of the struggling horses, and when that was done, we mounted and rode swiftly away.

We had learned that many white men traveled the roads, that it was not wise to linger long after the slaughter was finished.

Tired of the white woman's screaming, Red Willow pulled a hank of her long hair around until it filled her mouth. I glanced at her as I rode up beside him. There was blood on her mouth from biting her lips. Her eyes were wide, stark with terror. Her gaze lingered on my face and her eyes flickered oddly when they met my own.

You are white! they said in bewilderment. You must be white, for there are no blue eyes among the Indians.

I drummed on my horse's sides with my heels until he forged ahead. Yet behind me I could feel those great, terrified eyes upon me, without hope, yet wondering, wondering. . . .

I had thought the battle won when I refrained from plunging the Pawnee knife into Red Willow's back. Now I knew it was not won. I must fight it until all life was gone from the body of the white woman, and after that I knew I would fight a sour sickness of soul for many months to follow.

Who can understand such torment of mind that has not experienced it? My head whirled until I was dizzy. One moment I was Indian, feeding the flames of my hatred for the whites, recalling every wrong they had done us. The next I was white, knowing compassion for the white woman, knowing the wrong that was about to be done to her.

Well did I remember the words of Ha-sananen as he spoke to me atop the long ridge where I had gone to fast: "Revere the good you find in men and do not condemn when you discover bad as well."

I asked myself in desperation, Would Ha-sananen countenance what is about to be done? Would he ask me not to condemn this?

178

My heart told me he would not. No, I must stop it somehow. I must stop it.

Warfare and my Indian training had made me crafty enough to realize I could not stop my comrades with words. Nor could I fight them all and expect anything but defeat and loss of my life as well. It must be planned, and carefully. It must be done when night fell down upon the land, when pursuit would be difficult and escape possible. It must be done before the woman was stripped and staked out upon the ground.

Now my mind had something upon which to work. The torment had gone with decision, and I began feverishly to plan.

The miles flowed beneath the hoofs of our horses. In the lead, I headed toward some breaks in the open country that I knew. Upon the hills of the breaks grew dark cedars and pines. In the gullies were deep washes. Here, I thought, we would camp for the night. Here I would make my escape with the woman, for here would be many hiding places past which my comrades might well ride unseeing.

We reached the breaks and entered them, and the sun dropped behind a bank of clouds to the west. Red Willow tied the woman, who was silent now and near unconsciousness from exhaustion and fear. He ran his hand under her dress, made a lewd remark, and howled with laughter.

Others were gathering firewood, enough for a

big fire, since we had put many miles between ourselves and the burned coach. They could afford to be careless.

From their carelessness was born my plan. I allowed myself to wander away from the camp site, leading my horse, until I was out of sight. I tied him to a tree, and, creeping silently, circled the camp site until I was opposite the place where I had tied my horse.

This was the time. My nerves were tight to the breaking point. I was shivering. I raised and fired my gun. Immediately I let out a yell into which I tried to put pain, surprise, and alarm. I shouted, "White men! Four of them! Help me, for I am wounded!"

Scarcely had the last word left my lips than I was running, more silently, more swiftly than I had ever run before. I circled the camp, hearing the sounds of my comrades' approach, and avoiding them with all the skill I could muster.

I came up on the camp from the other side. I seized the white woman, clapped a hand over her mouth to stifle her startled scream, and ran with her for my horse.

I flung her over his withers like the inert carcass of a deer. Quickly I ripped away a part of her dress and stuffed it into her mouth. I mounted behind her and eased the horse away, keeping to soft ground and holding him in so that for the moment, at least, we might remain undiscovered.

For the first three hundred yards, there was only silence behind me. Then I heard the sharp bark of a coyote, another, and yet another. I had covered a full quarter mile before I heard the first howl of surprise.

They were shouting at one another, "Where is Sharp Knife? Is this a joke? There are no white men here. Have you seen him, Many Elks?"

One of them must have returned to camp and found the woman gone, for his voice rose, full of wild and uncontrolled anger: "He has betrayed us! He has stolen our prize! Track him down and kill him, for he is no Arapaho. He is a white and has revealed himself at last!"

Many Elks answered, "You are mistaken. He is teasing us. I know Sharp Knife. My brother would not betray us."

A sudden pang of regret struck me at his words, and for the first time I realized fully what I was giving up. For a moment I was tempted to turn around, to say it had been a joke.

The woman before me was whimpering softly, like a child, behind the gag I had placed in her mouth. Her body quivered like that of a frightened fawn. Looking at her, I knew I could not turn back.

I urged my horse into a run. Leaning forward, I spoke into her ear in English: "Don't be afraid. You're safe with me. I'll return you to your people unhurt."

Her head turned and I could feel her wide eyes watching me. I said, "When we have put a little distance behind us, I'll raise you up so you'll be more comfortable."

The trembling subsided but it didn't stop.

I put my mind to the business of escaping, and for a while I nearly forgot the woman. Watching a bank of clouds in the west before me, I uttered a soft prayer to Ha-sananen to make them spread and cover the stars, which might reveal my trail to those behind.

Ha-sananen must have smiled on me, because, while the clouds did not spread, I had put a mile between us before the faint cries of my comrades announced that they had found the trail. And I knew that now I was relatively safe. I could travel faster than they could follow. The moon would not rise for nearly four hours.

I stopped long enough to raise the woman, untie her, and put her astride the horse in front of me. Then, with one hand holding the reins, the other around her waist, I urged my horse on at a pace I knew he could maintain all night and still be alive, though barely so, in the morning.

III. THE DISMAL GLORY

Chapter Thirteen

IN THE FIRST GRAY LIGHT of dawn, I paused long enough to search the land behind from a high promontory. I was intensely relieved when I saw nothing. Before me the woman was slumped, mercifully asleep at last.

My horse now traveled with his head down, and his hide was wet and gleaming with sweat.

I had pushed him hard throughout the night, sparing him only enough to keep him alive and traveling. An Indian grows to know exactly the strength and endurance of a horse, gains the ability to ration it out to the last wheeze of breath, to the last possible mile at the greatest possible speed.

I'd had the whole night to consider what I'd done, and now, in the cold light of morning, I was sick with regret. Two Antelopes had been right and his curse had been strong. I could not go back to the Arapaho, nor would the white men welcome me. I was known. I was Sharp Knife. The lieutenant of cavalry would remember me, and upon my shoulders he would heap the blame for the killing of his men. Others among the whites, knowing what the men of White Otter's band had done, would know as well what I had done.

I faced another hazard, a more immediate one. I was an Indian, carrying a captured white woman across my saddle. If I were to be seen, no questions would be asked. I would be shot down like a marauding wolf.

My only hope, then, was to ride cautiously to the outskirts of the town called Denver, there to release the woman. Then I must leave, must ride away, forsaking the white, forsaken by the Arapaho. Alone would I travel, alone would I live until one day I was set upon by those who had been my brothers, and then I would be killed.

At sunup the woman stirred. Looking around at me, she began to cry hysterically.

I spoke softly. "Don't be afraid of me. I'm white myself. When I was nine I was captured by the Arapaho and raised by them."

She quieted. Her face was drawn, tired. I knew she was exhausted. After a while she asked wearily, "What's your name?"

I was surprised to realize I didn't remember my white name. It had been too long. I said, "I don't know my white name. Among the Arapaho, I am Sharp Knife."

"What will you do now? You can't go back to them."

"I know I can't. Neither can I go to the whites. My name is known to them. I wear four of their scalps at my belt."

She shuddered. Her eyes were wide and wondering as they looked at my face.

I asked, "What are you called?"

"Dorothy. Dorothy Webb."

"It's a nice name." I repeated her name twice. "What does it mean?"

"Mean?"

"Indian names have meaning. Sharp Knife, Many Elks, Singing Wind." Saying the last, I felt a sharp pang, a bitter sense of loss.

The girl smiled faintly for the first time. "Names have meanings among the whites, too, but most of the meanings have been forgotten. I don't know what Dorothy means."

"You have a husband in Denver? A father and mother?"

"A father." Her forehead furrowed. "He'll be frantic with worry when he gets news of the coach."

"Perhaps we'll reach Denver ahead of the news."

"You think we might? That would be wonderful." But her tone disproved her words. Right now, nothing was wonderful to her. Terror had taken too great a toll.

The girl looked much younger than I, and I guessed she was eighteen or nineteen. Her hair, tangled and dusty, yet managed to be more beautiful than anything I had ever seen before.

Indians respect strength in women. There was no strength at all in this one. She was weak and wholly helpless. Yet her weakness stirred no contempt in me. Instead I felt a surge of protective compassion, and told myself I would guard her well, would deliver her safely to her people in Denver. And when she was gone, what then?

Suddenly I was alone, more terribly so than I had ever been in my life before. Never could I return to my friends, never again would I see the face of Singing Wind. For the sake of a woman I had never seen before, would never see again, I had made my choice. The wrongness of it was like gall in my mouth, a bitter, acrid taste.

Yet had I not intervened, this girl would be dead.

All that day we traveled. When the sun was high in the sky, I gave her a little of the pemmican from my parfleche and she chewed it, with distaste at first, afterward hungrily.

We halted at a stream and I discovered she could not even drink from it. She cupped her hands and drank from them instead.

She was very dirty, very tired, but she was lovely in spite of that. Her fear of me had left and we talked of a great many things.

"I owe you my life," she said once. "More than

my life. I owe you more than I can ever repay. My father has money and influence in Denver. He'll see that nobody bothers you. It's the least we can do."

I shook my head. "I wouldn't get ten feet inside the town before somebody took a shot at me."

"Then we'll change your appearance. You're a white man, not an Indian."

Easier said than done. I smiled at her. Her idea was foolish, but she was nice for having it.

My horse was tiring. All spring had gone from his step, and he plodded listlessly, stumbling often. I knew I would be lucky if he lasted out the thirty miles that yet remained to be traveled. I said nothing about his condition to the girl, who seemed not to have noticed it. But I kept my eyes busy, looking for a ranch, a farmhouse, a stagecoach station from which I could steal another.

The hours dragged, and all day I watched my back trail, thinking hopefully that perhaps they wouldn't catch me at all. Their horses were as tired as mine, and unless they stole fresh ones . . .

The sun sank slowly toward the mountains, which were clearer now, higher, less shrouded with haze. And at sundown I sighted a small collection of shacks on the horizon before me.

Keeping to low country so as not to be skylined, I rode toward them and dismounted when I was about a mile away. I lifted Dorothy down and told her, "I need a fresh horse. This one will die before the night is over."

"How do you expect to get a fresh horse, away out here?"

I smiled at her, wondering how the whites could be so powerful and yet so unseeing, so helpless as this one was, as so many others among them were.

I said, "There are some buildings ahead of us. I'll steal a horse there."

"Please. Won't this one do? Stealing will only get you into trouble, and besides, it's wrong."

"It's also wrong to let my comrades catch us and kill us, which they're sure to do if I don't get a fresh horse."

"You won't . . ." She hesitated. "You won't hurt anyone?"

"They won't even see me or hear me." I moved away. "Wait."

I stopped and looked back. She said, reversing herself with feminine logic, "As long as you're going to steal a horse, you might as well steal some clothes too. White men's clothes."

"If I can."

As I traveled, I considered what she had said. Perhaps she was right. Maybe I could change myself so as to appear white, and if I could do that, maybe I could find a place among the whites. They need not know who I was.

I pictured myself living among the whites, and

did not like the picture. Among the whites you had to pay for the lodge in which you slept, your food, your clothes. Before you could pay, you had to have money, and to get it you must work at one of the many silly and useless occupations at which white men worked.

Deep in my thoughts, I approached the group of buildings, covering most of the distance hidden in a shallow ravine. When I was within three hundred yards of the buildings, I lay down on my belly and crawled out to a spot from which I could watch.

The gray of dusk had settled over the place. Lamplight winked from the dirty windows of the largest building. A man came out of it and walked to a small square building in the rear. A few moments later he reappeared, hitching up his pants. I waited until he had gone back.

It was now almost dark. Moving like a wraith and keeping to the shadows, I went toward the cluster of buildings.

I avoided the large, lighted one, and went among the smaller ones, where I found a pole corral containing many horses.

Most of them were large, like those that pulled the stagecoaches. But a few were smaller, like the fleet ponies of the Indians. I selected the strongest-looking of these and went in to get him.

The horses milled around in fear, but soon

quieted when I spoke soothing words to them in English. I slipped my hair rope around the neck of the one I had selected, a trim sorrel. I led him through the gate and closed it behind me. Mounting, I rode the horse away from the buildings and tied him to a clump of brush. Then afoot I returned again.

This would not be so simple as stealing the horse had been. I must employ a ruse to draw the whites from their lighted house.

I opened the corral gate and shooed the horses out, only this time I did not soothe them, since I wanted their noise to be heard. They ran, kicked, bucked, and snorted. A shout rose from the doorway of the large building, which I judged was a stagecoach station. Immediately afterward three whites came from the doorway. There were a young man and a woman, besides the man I had seen before.

They followed the horses, shouting foolishly and uselessly. The one I had seen go into the small square building cursed in a way that made me remember Sonofabitch Smith.

Quickly I went inside and glanced around. The smell of the place was strong from cooking food. I heard movement in the kitchen and drew the Pawnee knife. With it clutched in my hand, I crossed the room.

There was a woman in the kitchen. A glance told me she was not white, but Indian. She looked around at me and her eyes went flat with fear.

She was fat, and old by my standards. I spoke in Arapaho. "Make one noise and I will cut your throat." Her eyes told me she understood, so I went on: "I wish some of the clothes belonging to the white men. Give them to me quickly and be silent about it afterward or I will return and add your scalp to those already at my belt."

She nodded, unspeaking, her eyes still holding that flat, dull look of fear. She went past me fearfully, as though not trusting the knife in my hand. From a tall box in the corner she took a pair of pants, a white shirt, and a pair of leather boots. I saw a hat I fancied hanging from a nail on the wall and took that too. Then with a final gesture of my forefinger across my throat and a cold warning glance, I departed.

Now quickly I ran to the place where I had tied the horse. Mounting him, I rode quietly back to the place where I had left Dorothy Webb.

I called out to reassure her, "It is Sharp Knife and I have a fine horse and some new clothes."

I dismounted. She made but a silent white blur against the night. I stripped off my leggings and breechclout, kicked off my moccasins. With the soft leather of my leggings I removed the war paint from my face and chest. Dorothy gasped, and seemed to draw away from me, but I paid her no attention, for I was donning the awkward white man's clothing.

The man they had belonged to must have been very near my size, for they fitted me well. The boots were awkward on my feet, and clumsy. No wonder white men made so much noise when they walked.

I was surprised to hear Dorothy giggling. I asked, irritated, "What are you laughing at? Do you think I'm funny?"

"Of course not. It isn't that. It's only . . . well, we'll have to cut your hair, that's all."

I realized I was wearing the white man's hat. I took it off and fingered my braids, which reached nearly halfway to my waist. I handed Dorothy the knife. "Cut it, then." She took the knife clumsily and began to cut my hair. The knife was sharp, and once she nicked my ear with it. The braids fell to the ground, and afterward she trimmed the hair until it lay close to my head after the fashion of the white men.

I put the hat on. "Does Sharp Knife look like a white man now?"

"Like none I've ever seen." She was still giggling. My irritable anger increased, and she must have sensed this, for she sobered at once. "You're more handsome than a white man. But if you're to wear the white man's clothes, you'll need a white man's name. My mother's name was Kelly. Do you like that?"

"Is it a woman's name?" I asked suspiciously.

"It fits both men and women." The laughter

was now gone from her voice. "William Kelly. How does that sound to you?"

"William is the name of a great friend of the Cheyenne. William Bent; I would be honored to use his name."

"All right. William Kelly it is, then."

I retained my rifle and the Pawnee knife, nothing else. With considerable regret I buried my braids, my clothing, my trophies and weapons in the ground at my feet. I transferred my bridle to the captured horse and released my own Indian pony. I lifted Dorothy up and mounted behind her.

At a fast pace we went around the buildings of the stage station and headed toward Denver.

Chapter Fourteen

I WAS AMAZED at the size of Denver, at the way it had grown in the few short months since I'd been here before. There must have been as many whites now living in this one place as there were Indians in both the Arapaho and Cheyenne tribes.

Buildings were arranged in neat squares with wooden pathways all around. Many of the buildings were dark, but in others lamplight shone out through the windows.

Dorothy directed me to pause near a stooped old man and asked him where she would find the Planter's House. By pointing and terse directions, he told her, and presently we drew up before an enormous building with light gleaming from half a hundred windows. I lifted her down and tied the horse to a railing before the place. As though she belonged here, she went inside, while I followed somewhat fearfully at her heels.

I stared around me in awe. The floor was flat as the surface of a lake, and made of some white material laid in a wondrous pattern. Above me hung chandeliers made of glass like jewels, which reflected light like the morning sun upon the dewy grass.

I noticed the stares of the whites all around me

and put my hand on the hilt of the Pawnee knife. If they attacked me now, I was lost. But I would take many of them with me when I died.

They did not attack. They only stared, and moved uneasily away.

I heard a hoarse shout, a tortured cry, "Dorothy!" and then a white-haired old man was running through the crowd toward us. He flung his arms around her. Tears ran unashamedly across his cheeks and lost themselves in his trimmed white beard. "Oh, my God! Thank God! We got the news, and I thought you were dead— or worse."

Dorothy was crying too. When she could speak, she turned to me and said, "I would be dead but for Mr. Kelly, here."

The man looked at me. His face was fleshy and red, his body thick and short. But his eyes were sharp, kind, and grateful too. He grasped my hand and pumped it up and down.

As he studied me, his grasp grew suddenly limp. I could feel the sweat leap into his palm where it touched mine. His face grew pale, his eyes wide and panicky. He looked as though he had just discovered a bear dressed in man's clothes. He whispered, "My God, Dorothy! This is no white man!"

I dropped his hand. My own stole toward the handle of my knife. I knew what he was going to do, knew I had to stop him before he did it.

Dorothy stepped between us. I had not seen strength in her before, but I saw it now. She spoke sharply, in a very low voice. "Father! Get hold of yourself. He saved my life, do you understand? He saved my life!"

She grasped him by the arm, clutched me with her other hand. She said, "We can't talk here. Which room is yours, Father?"

He gave her a number in a scared, shocked voice. The three of us went up the ornate, curving stairway and down a long hall. Dorothy's father opened a door and Dorothy pushed us inside the room. She closed the door behind.

"Now you listen to me! This man is as white as you are, but he's been with the Indians since he was nine. He rescued me from them at the risk of his own life. By doing so, he made enemies of them and can't go back. He needs a place among the whites and I'm going to see that you give it to him. Is that clear?"

She had said that her father was very powerful among the whites, but he didn't look powerful now. He nodded weakly.

The girl went on: "This man's band is at war with the whites. He has killed at least four white men. I saw their scalps myself. So you see, if it's discovered who he is . . . Well, you know as well as I do what would happen to him. It's up to us to see that he's accepted as a white man—which he is."

Her father looked at me furtively, still sweating. He said, "But, Dorothy, he's a killer! He's more Indian than white!"

My anger was stirring now, and no doubt it showed in my eyes. Dorothy lost color, but she gave no ground. "He understands English as well as you do, Father. Try to remember that. And he saved my life. Doesn't that mean anything to you?"

"But four men! How do we know—"

"There won't be more?" Dorothy stamped her foot. "All of us are only what we've been taught to be. Would you call one of our Union soldiers a killer because he had killed four Rebels in battle? Would a frontier soldier be a killer because he had killed four Indians?" Her color was high now and she was very angry.

The old man was stubborn. "But murder—"

I said coldly, "It was not murder. Our band is at war with the white men. They have taken our land in violation of their own treaties."

Dorothy's voice was shaking now. She was near hysteria, from weariness, from hunger, from her experiences of the past two days. She said, "It was not only my *life* he saved. Do you know how a white woman dies among the Indians, Father?"

He sat down abruptly, trembling. "What do you want me to do?"

"That's better." She looked at him thoughtfully. "His name is William Kelly. According to your letter, you're having trouble getting your coaches through. All right. Give him a job as guard. If I know him the coach he's riding will get through."

Webb nodded. "All right." He was grinning a little now, ruefully. "Anything else?"

"Yes. He's not used to things. Get him a room. Go with him while he eats. Explain to him about money, and give him some. Then let him sleep about twelve hours. He needs it even worse than I do."

She sank down on the bed. I noticed how drawn her face was, how dull her eyes were. She was exhausted, but she hadn't given in until she'd repaid her debt to me. I grinned at her and she smiled back. Then Webb said, "Come on, Kelly. We'll eat."

He took me downstairs and out of the hotel. We went into a small steamy building that smelled of cooking. We sat down upon stools at a long counter. Webb ordered something to be sent up to Dorothy first. Then he ordered for us.

I sat staring around me in pure wonder. There was red-and-white checked cloth on all the tables and at the windows. There were lamps that gave off much light hanging from the walls. There were dishes with beautiful designs on them, and bright silver implements to eat with. Most wonderful of all were the vessels they gave us with water in them, for they were clear as the water itself, but hard and cold.

The food was strange, but very good. I was ravenous, and ate quickly. Afterward Webb gave me a cigar, which I lighted, watching him to see how it was done.

Perhaps, I thought, there was good in the white man's way of life. It was certainly easy, at least. When you were hungry, you simply went into one of these buildings, of which there were many, and told them what you wanted. When you wished to sleep, you found a hotel, and they let you use a room with a bed in it.

When we had finished eating, Webb gave something to the woman who had served us, and we left. We went back to the hotel, and he spoke to a man in the lobby. The man led us up the stairs to a room similar to the one Webb had.

I went in and they closed the door behind me. I stood my rifle in a corner and looked around.

I sat down on the bed, but it was too soft for my liking. So I took a blanket from it and lay down on the floor. I was instantly asleep.

I slept neither soundly nor well. Each small noise awakened me, and I would lie still with my hand on my knife until memory came flooding back, until I recalled that I was no longer Sharp Knife the Arapaho, but William Kelly the white man. Then I would return to my uneasy sleep.

I awoke at dawn, rose, and went to the window. In the village of White Otter, there would have been movement and activity at this hour. In the town of the white men, there was none, save for that of a solitary man, drunk on medicine water, staggering along in the middle of the road.

I was thirsty. There was a white vessel containing water on a small table in my room, and I drank from it. In what remained, I washed.

The hotel was completely silent. I remembered the late-rising caravan we had attacked a couple of years before, and guessed that this was the way of the white men. They rose late in the morning, and stayed up late in the night.

I was depressed and discouraged. So many things were strange to me. The people were strange. I had no friends save Dorothy Webb and her father, and I was not sure I could count her father a friend.

Perhaps, too, Dorothy was promised in marriage. Oddly, the thought depressed me even further.

I lay down on the bed and closed my eyes. In my mind I saw Singing Wind, her lithe body, her beautiful dark eyes and smiling mouth.

I was a fool! What was the life of one white woman worth? Was it worth this? Was it a fair trade for a man's way of life, for his friends, for the woman he loved more than life itself?

I should have let my comrades have the girl. I could have ridden back to the village alone so that I would not have had to hear, to watch.

I got up and paced the floor, fighting out my torment of mind. The sun came up and shone through the window of my room, and now I could hear the beginning of activity in the street below.

Still I did not go out, for I did not want to face my new life. I feared the white men, and hated them. I feared that if I did go out, I would become involved in a fight with them, and I knew that if I were, I would be killed. They were too many for me, and I was alone among them.

A knocking on my door startled me. I drew the Pawnee knife, and with it ready in my hand, flung open the door.

Dorothy's father stood in the hall. He saw my face and the knife, and shrank away from me. I returned it to the sheath.

He said, "Don't be so damned touchy, Kelly. Nobody's going to hurt you. You're among friends. Let them alone and they'll let you alone."

I could feel my body relax. I said, "I'm hungry."

"Sure. That's what I came for. Come on, we'll eat. Then I'll take you down to the stage depot and show you around. Dorothy's not up yet, and likely won't be till noon."

"All right." I followed him out and down the stairs. We ate breakfast at the same place where we'd eaten the night before, and afterward walked toward the river.

At the edge of town was a large corral in which were many horses and half a dozen stagecoaches.

There was a small building near the gate, and we went into this.

Behind a desk sat a huge, bearded man about my age, dressed in buckskins. Webb said, "Jimmy, this is William Kelly. He's to ride guard for us."

Jimmy got up and stuck out a hairy paw. I took it, knowing that this was one of the white men's customs. Jimmy gripped my hand briefly, studying my face. He said, "Been with the Injuns, ain't he?"

Webb looked surprised. "Why, yes, as a matter of fact he has. He speaks English, but that's about all. The Arapaho have had him since he was nine. He's the one that rescued my daughter from them."

Jimmy squinted at me. "How come?"

"How come?"

Webb said, "He means why? Why did you rescue her?"

I shrugged. "I don't know. She was screaming, and I knew I had to stop it, that's all."

Jimmy still peered at me as though he were looking right into my mind. "Don't like white men, do you?"

"No. How did you know?"

"Guessed. Was I an Injun, I reckon I'd feel the same way."

I liked him. It was one of those things that comes over you occasionally upon meeting a

203

stranger. Webb said, "He's wild. He's like a cornered wolf most of the time, ready to fight at the drop of a hat. Watch him, Jimmy. Don't let him kill anyone."

Jimmy grunted, "I'll try. You want him to go out right away?"

Webb nodded. "Sooner the better. I don't want Dorothy to—well, you know."

"Yeah. All right, Mr. Webb."

"And Jimmy, I know you're busy. But he doesn't understand about money or anything. Give him a month's pay and take him uptown to get what clothes he needs. Talk to him a little so he'll kind of begin to get used to things."

"Sure. It'll be a pleasure."

Webb went out and closed the door behind him. Jimmy went to an iron box, a safe, in the corner and took out two gold coins. He gave them to me. "Bill, this is a month's pay. Forty bucks. It'll be all you'll get for four weeks."

"Weeks?"

"A week's seven days. Four times seven days. Then you get two more." He began to chuckle. "Damned if that don't sound cheesy. Two little pieces of metal for a month's work. You'd rather get somethin' you could eat or wear or fight with, wouldn't you?"

I didn't understand him always, but I liked the sound of his voice. I trusted him, even more than I had Webb.

He said, "Come on. Let's go uptown."

I followed him. We walked into the town and he took me first to a store filled with clothes. When we came out, I was newly outfitted from head to foot. "Can't never tell when the monkey that owns them duds will spot 'em on you. Safest thing is to get rid of 'em."

There was wisdom in that. He looked at my rifle. "Hell, we'll get rid of that next. Come on."

We went into another store where guns were sold. After some haggling, Jimmy traded my rifle in on a revolving rifle, a scarce and valuable gun, as I later learned. He also purchased one of the revolving short guns and a belt and holster for me. He said, "Half the trouble we're in is because our drivers an' guards ain't armed the best we kin arm 'em. One-shot rifles ain't no good when you're up on a box with fifteen-twenty Injuns howlin' all around you. This way, you got enough shots to clear 'em off without reloadin'."

A new thought seemed to occur to him and he looked at me oddly. "Webb didn't think of it, likely, but how you gonna feel about killin' Injuns?"

"I will not attack them. If they attack me, I'll defend myself."

"Good. You got any squaws, Bill?"

"Arapaho men do not marry young. I have a sweetheart."

205

"Yeah? What's her name?"

"Waanibe. Singing Wind."

"You gave her up an' saved Webb's girl? Well, I reckon he owes you more'n he'll ever pay. Anyhow, the guns are on him, an' by God, the duds too. That forty's all yours. We'll get it changed, so's you'll have somethin' to jingle in your pockets."

We went into a saloon, where Jimmy ordered beer for both of us. I tasted it, but I did not like its bite or its bitterness. I left my glass untouched and Jimmy did not urge me to drink it. The bartender changed my gold pieces into silver, a great deal of it.

When we got back to the stage depot, Dorothy was there. She looked at me with approval, and smiled. "Getting used to things?"

"A little."

"You look fine in your new clothes." She was shy with me, and did not seem to know what to say. Jimmy tactfully went into the small building and closed the door. Dorothy looked up at me and a faint flush stained her face. Her glance fell away from mine.

I said, "You look rested and fresh again. You are very pretty."

"Thank you." Her color had deepened. "Dad says you're going out on the eastbound stage this afternoon."

I shrugged. I hadn't heard, but I didn't care. It

was what I was supposed to do in return for the money Jimmy had given me. I said, "At least I won't have to stay inside and work, as so many white men do. At least I'll be outside in the open air."

"Yes." She looked at me thoughtfully. "You're not happy with the exchange you made, are you?"

I understood her, but pretended not to. "I don't know what you mean."

"You miss your Indian friends."

I was silent.

"Do you have a wife?"

"I have a sweetheart—or I had one. I'll never see her again now. My Indian father is dead, but my Indian mother still lives. She will go to live in one of the lodges of her relatives now, since I'm no longer there to care for her."

I was surprised to discover tears in Dorothy's eyes. "I owe you so much—so very much."

"You owe me nothing. I did what my heart told me I had to do. If it hadn't been you, it would have been someone else at some other time."

"Yes. I suppose it would. Could I ask you a question?" I nodded.

"Was . . . was that the way your mother died— at the hands of the Indians? Is that why . . ." She halted. She took an involuntary step away from me. Her eyes turned wide with fright.

I regained control of myself with difficulty. I

said, "Yes. I suppose that's why I couldn't stand your screams."

"I'm sorry. I'm terribly sorry."

"It's all past now. There's no need to be sorry. I don't hate the Indians for what they did. They have wiped out bitterness with kindness. Besides, what they did is no worse than some things the white men do."

Dorothy looked surprised. "I never thought of it that way."

"No. Often the white people don't think. For one thing, they don't realize, most of them, that they are invaders, trespassers. They think of this land as theirs for the taking. But it's not. It belongs to us. If only they would realize that. If only they would try to understand the Indians." I stopped. I had spoken heatedly. I said, "But you can have no interest in that."

"But I do. I do. And I think that if you could learn to control that temper of yours, you could do a lot to improve relations between Indians and whites."

"My temper?"

She smiled at me teasingly. "Every time something doesn't please you, your hand goes to that knife."

I shrugged, strangely irritated.

She said, "White men do a lot of fighting among themselves. But they don't fight to the death. You must learn that."

"I suppose so. Indians are different. Rarely do they quarrel among themselves. When they do, one of them dies."

"Is there no punishment for killing?"

"In a fight? No, if the reason for the fight is strong, and if the fight has been fair."

We might have continued the conversation, but at that moment Webb arrived. He looked angry when he saw Dorothy and me talking together. He growled, "I don't like to see you hanging around down here, Dorothy. It's not safe."

I said, "She's safe when she's with me."

"Of course. Of course." But he was still irritated. He sent me into the building to ask Jimmy to come out, but when I returned outside with him, both Webb and Dorothy were gone.

I was puzzled. Jimmy grinned at me ruefully. "How the hell am I going to explain that to you?"

"Explain what?"

"About the boss's daughter. Look, Bill. Even among the Injuns, I reckon a father tries to get the best man he can for his daughter, don't he?"

"Yes."

Jimmy shifted uneasily. "Well, to lay it out on the line cold, I reckon Webb don't think you're the best he can get. You understand?"

I was suddenly angry. I said, "I understand."

He said, "Good enough to save her life, but not good enough to come courtin'. That's the deal, Bill. It's one of the rotten things about the system, but there it is. Neither you nor I am goin' to change it."

I was angry and lonely, and hurt to discover I was not thought good enough for the girl Dorothy. I said, "Sharp Knife has been a fool. He should have closed his ears and stayed with his friends."

"Don't take it thataway, now. An' don't sell that girl short. She's all wool an' a yard wide. You just wait an' see." He turned and walked away, muttering to himself.

And I sat down to wait until it would be time to mount the box of the stagecoach for the long trip east.

Chapter Fifteen

THE COACH WAS READY about three hours before sunset. I mounted to my seat beside the driver and acknowledged Jimmy's friendly wave, and we rolled out of the yard and up through the town.

We halted before the Planter's House, waiting for the eastbound stage from the mountains. I looked up and saw Dorothy waving to me from her window. I waved back.

Then the coach from the mountains drew up in a cloud of dust, and the passengers began to alight. They went into the hotel for a short rest, and afterward came out and got into our coach. There were three men and a small boy.

The driver, beside me, was a frowning, sour-faced man named Jeff Bekins. He yelled at his teams, popped his long whip above their heads, and set them galloping, letting them gain speed as we left the limits of the town. When they had run off their nervousness, he drew them in to the pace they could maintain until they were changed at the first way station.

Then he looked at me. "I don't know why I always draw the dirty jobs, Injun, but I drew you. So let's understand each other right off.

Webb says you're white, an' mebbe you are. But you don't look white to me. Anyways, if we git jumped, this here gun's goin' to be in your ribs while yours is pointin' at the redskins. You make one bad move an' it's goin' to blow your guts out. That clear to you?"

I snarled, "It's clear," and those were the last words I spoke to him all through the night. Like strangers, like enemies we rode on the bouncing seat, while my blood ran alternately hot and cold. I wanted to kill him for his nastiness, for his suspicion. Yet I was forced to ride beside him, saying nothing, doing nothing.

A dozen times I considered leaping from the seat, losing myself in the vast plain, every inch of which was familiar to me. Would it not be better, I asked myself, to wander alone on the plain, living as I have always lived, than to wander alone among the white men, suspected and distrusted?

And then I remembered Dorothy's words: "If you could learn to control that temper of yours, you could do a lot to improve relations between Indians and whites."

Remembering her words, and the girl herself, I stayed on the seat, and rode out the night in silence.

All the next day we drove, and the next. After that we had a day's rest, and then we began the return trip.

Jeff Bekins spoke to me only when it was necessary to tell me what to do. It was "Here, Kelly, git down an' grab them valises. Throw 'em in the boot." Or "Take over fer a while, but no tricks. I'll be watchin' you."

Both trips were made without incident. And five days after leaving, we rolled back into Denver City.

After discharging our passengers at the Planter's House, we drove to the corral at the edge of town. Pulling up before the gate, Bekins looked down at Jimmy, who stood on the ground, grinning at me, holding the gate open so Bekins could drive in. Bekins said, "By Jesus, this is my last run, less'n you give me a white man fer a guard. I ain't ridin' with this goddamn Injun again."

The grin went out of Jimmy's eyes. He said, "Get down, Bill. Let Jeff drive in. The hostlers will take care of the horses."

I got down. Bekins drove through the gate. Jimmy asked, "What happened?"

"Nothing. Nothing happened. He just doesn't trust me, that's all."

"I was afraid of that." Jimmy was silent for a moment. Then he said, "Drivers like Bekins are scarce. I'll try you on the run west into the mountains."

He did. He tried me on that run, and on the one south, and on the one north to Fort Laramie. It was always the same. I wasn't a white man to the

213

drivers I rode with, but an Indian who could not be trusted.

Many times during that winter I remembered Two Antelopes' dying curse. Many times I recalled the way my Arapaho friends had looked at me, wondering, saying, "Do not trust that one. He will turn against us."

I had turned against them. Their suspicion had been justified. Perhaps the suspicions of the white men were also justified. Perhaps I would turn against them when the test came, just as I had turned against the Indians.

Somehow the winter passed, and in the spring the Colorado volunteers marched south to meet General Sibley's forces at La Glorieta Pass. I had tried to join them, feeling that if I could distinguish myself fighting for the white men of the North, perhaps they would accept me. But I was refused. Again it was a matter of trust.

So I stayed on in Denver, reduced now to a hostler, caring for the horses, cleaning and repairing coaches, shoveling manure from reeking stables. Dorothy had returned to the East to finish her schooling, so I did not even have the comfort of her presence to sustain me.

I will admit that I grew very bitter. Scowling and silent, I went about my work, avoiding my fellow workers and avoided by them.

At last, in 1862, Dorothy returned from the East.

I will not soon forget the experience of opening the coach door and seeing her step out. Instantly her face lighted. Instantly a glad cry sprang from her lips. "Bill!" And then her arms were around my neck.

All the loneliness I had felt, all the hunger I had known were in the way my arms tightened around her. She was soft, and warm, and fragrantly feminine. She raised her face to me, wonder shining from her eyes, and I lowered my lips to hers.

It was to have been a light kiss of welcome, a brief greeting, for I had learned my place painfully over the past six or seven months. Yet when my lips touched hers, something happened within me. My arms tightened fiercely around her warm body. Bruisingly my mouth came down over hers.

Not for an instant was she startled or withdrawing. As though she had waited as long as I for this, she clung to me, matching my passion with her own.

Breathless, at last she drew away. In her eyes I saw a look that reminded me of Singing Wind. Completely unconscious of those around us, she cried, "Bill! Oh, Bill, I've missed you so! How have you been and what have you been doing? Are you still riding guard?"

All the wonder fled from the moment. I could feel my face settling into a pattern of bitterness.

I said, "I am a hostler at the corrals. I take care of the horses and the coaches. I sleep in the tack room near the corral gate."

"But why? I thought—"

"To the drivers I'm still an Indian. They're afraid to trust themselves to me. They think that if Indians attack, I'll betray them."

"Oh, no!" Her face flushed with anger. Her lips firmed with determination. "I didn't know, Bill. You never wrote."

I said, "I don't know how to write."

"You will. I'll teach you myself. Come on, Bill. Bring my bags. You and I are going to talk to Father . . . Some things are going to get changed."

I said stiffly, "I want no favors I haven't earned."

"Nonsense. Nobody's going to give you any favors. When I needed help, you gave it. Now it's my turn. The only thing I'm sorry for is that I haven't given it sooner." And so, over the strenuous objections of her father, Dorothy began to teach me to write.

No longer did I work at the corral on the western edge of town. Instead, I began working in the stageline office.

The summer passed, and the winter, and now I could read the newspaper and follow the progress of settlement in Colorado, could follow the deterioration of relations between Indians and whites. Fear of the Indians was rampant following terrible massacres of whites by the Sioux in Minnesota, for the Cheyenne and Arapaho were known to be friends of the Sioux. And the white man's forts in Colorado were poorly manned and poorly equipped because of the demands of their war with the South.

As well they were frightened, perhaps, for they began to speak softly, to walk carefully in their dealings with the tribes. And because they did, incidents were few.

Eighteen-sixty-three came. I could read skillfully and write well now. And Dorothy, ever insistent that I better myself, began to bring me books about the white man's law, which interested me greatly and which I devoured as fast as she could get them.

We were close—almost as close as Singing Wind and I had been. We took drives in the early evening. We attended plays and concerts. Not since that first kiss as she stepped from the stagecoach had I touched Dorothy, except for an occasional brushing of hands by accident. In spite of that, I had my plans. I had studied long and well. Soon I would be ready to take my place among the whites as a lawyer. There would be, I knew, many months before they would completely accept me, before I would earn enough to take a wife. But when I could . . .

In the meantime I treated Dorothy only as a good friend, though there were times when my pulse pounded at her nearness, when I burned to take her in my arms, to carry her from the buggy in which we rode and lay her down in some grassy clump of trees, there to know her completely, to make her my own. But I had learned restraint among the Arapaho, and I practiced it now.

Perhaps Dorothy was practicing it too, for she grew pale and lost a great deal of weight. There were times when I would catch her watching me furtively, with as much longing and hunger in her eyes as was in my heart. And now there was something else in her eyes, a kind of puzzled hurt, as though she were asking, Why? Why do you do nothing? Don't you want me? Can't you forget Singing Wind? Are you planning to leave me and go back to the Indians?

The summer passed, and bad weather forced abandonment of our evening drives. Dorothy grew distant with me, as though she had erected a wall between us to protect herself from the hurt of frustration.

Speak, I told myself. Tell her you want her. But now it was too late and she gave me no opportunity, taking care never to allow herself to be alone with me.

That winter saw the end of what little friend-liness had existed between Indians and whites. In the spring Lieutenant George Eayre attacked a Cheyenne village on Ash Creek and killed seventeen. He returned in triumph to Denver, and when he marched again it was under orders to "kill Cheyenne whenever and wherever found."

Not until later did I learn that with eighty-four soldiers he had attacked five or six hundred Cheyenne. Had they not desired peace, they could have obliterated his command with little trouble. Yet the incident only strengthened the belief in Denver that one white soldier was equal to twenty savages.

And so it went. At Fort Wise, now renamed Fort Lyon, a new Indian agent named Colley was enriching himself by selling and trading Indian annuity goods to the very Indians to which they were supposed to be given.

Fear and distrust rode the land. And now the governor of the new territory of Colorado made an attempt to salvage the chances for peace. By proclamation he called on all friendly Kiowas and Comanches to go to Fort Larned on the Arkansas, all southern Cheyenne and Arapaho to go to Fort Lyon. There, if they would surrender their arms, they would be fed and clothed and protected from their enemies.

An earnest gesture, and it might have worked, except for the men who handled things from there on—Colley at Fort Lyon, a drunken captain in charge at Fort Larned; Colley dishonest, Captain Permeter contemptuous and rude.

Yet even so, owing mostly to the Indians' forbearance, the surrender was arranged. Black

Kettle and Left Hand promised that their people would gather just as soon as the summer medicine dances had been held.

But peace was not to be the fate of the tribes. Kiowas approaching Fort Larned were fired upon. The sentry was shot through the arm with an arrow. More ill feeling. A council was called at the fort, and the Kiowas, full of resentment, used the council as an opportunity to run off the fort's entire horse herd.

Left Hand, as always working for peace, approached the fort under a white flag to offer his services in recovering the horses from the Kiowas. Soldiers in the fort fired upon him and his party with a cannon.

No casualties. No wounded, no lives lost. Yet something infinitely more precious was lost. The tenuous thread of Indian patience was broken at last. Even Left Hand conceded that the whites did not want peace. He had given to the cause of peace all he would give. Now let there be war.

Webb's coaches stopped running after he lost six in a single week. No one dared ride them. Settlers flocked in from the plains and camped at the edge of Denver. Merchandise trains were plundered, and now when you saw a party of Indians in the distance, it was to discover that they all wore bright silk shirts, made by their squaws from bolts of stolen silk.

It was a war of extermination. Plumes of

smoke rose wherever there was a ranch or farm. Commerce with the East was at a standstill. Food in Denver became scarce, and prices rose. Flour went to twenty-five dollars a sack.

Summer passed, and fall came. William Bent, working feverishly, desperately now, arranged the surrender of some white captives by a village of Cheyenne. He persuaded some of the chiefs to come to Denver for a parley with Governor Evans. There, Evans scolded the chiefs for not having gone in to the two forts as they had promised.

A cruel joke, intentional or not. Yet even after all that had happened, 650 Arapaho went to Big Timbers and surrendered their arms, only to find that the promises of one white man, even the governor, were not necessarily binding upon the others. They were fed for ten days, then given their arms back and told to go out on the plain and live by hunting.

Black Kettle, heading a peace delegation of fifty warriors, came in next, to offer peace. He was told that the white chief at Fort Lyon had no authority to make peace, that he should go back out on the plain and wait. In the meantime, he was assured, he was under the protection of the fort.

Meanwhile the whites were preparing for war. An army of volunteers was being formed, to be led by Colonel Chivington, the Methodist elder who had so distinguished himself in the battle of La Glorieta Pass. Ninety-day volunteers, they could not have been gathered as a long-term deterrent to hostilities. This command could be forming only for the old, old purpose of "teaching the tribes a lesson."

Leave well enough alone, I told myself. This is no concern of yours.

Yet it was, and I knew it was. Somewhere on the plain was the village of White Otter, Beaver Woman, Singing Wind. Suppose it were their village, or Left Hand's village, that was to fall under Chivington's guns?

In the end, I went to Chivington and offered my services as guide and interpreter, for in this capacity I felt I could be most effective in preventing bloodshed.

Chivington was doubtful. But he talked to Webb, who vouched for my trustworthiness because he wanted me away from Denver, away from his daughter. Jimmy, now a member of the volunteers, also vouched for me, as did Dorothy herself. And so, finally convinced, Chivington signed me on.

Chapter Sixteen

SEPTEMBER SLIPPED AWAY, and part of October, while the air grew sharp and the cottonwood leaves along Cherry Creek and the Platte turned bright yellow and gold. Dark clouds scudded along the horizon, and wedges of ducks and geese filled the skies like the tenuous streamers of cobwebs undulating in the wind.

Chivington's army stirred like a slumbering giant as rumors sped through it that the time had come to move. And at last the orders to move did come. Move east to Bijou Creek, they said, and wait for Colonel Chivington.

Why did he not ride with us? And why Bijou Creek, when it was known there were no Indians there?

On the evening before we were to leave, I hired a buggy, bought a box lunch, and picked up Dorothy at the stageline office. Webb scowled at me as I helped her into the seat, but I pretended not to see.

I drove west to the Platte, and north, and halted the buggy in a golden grove of cottonwoods that had already shed enough leaves to carpet the ground softly with their brilliant color.

Dorothy seemed strange and withdrawn. I said, "You've been avoiding me. Why?"

"Have I? I wasn't aware of it."

A fast pulse beat in her throat, reminding me of the pulse that had beat there at the time of her capture by the Arapaho.

I said, "I will be gone for a month or two. When I return, I want to marry you."

For an instant she was very still. Tears filled her eyes and her lips began to tremble. Unsure of myself, I waited.

"Oh, why didn't you ask me sooner?" It was almost a cry of anguish. My heart sank. Was she promised to someone else? Had I waited too long?

I said stiffly, "I could neither read nor write. I was fit for nothing but to be a hostler in your father's stables. Could I have asked you to share that?"

"Yes. You could have asked. And I would have shared it, too."

"But you won't now?"

She was smiling through her tears. "Of course I will . . . Oh, Bill! Bill!"

She was in my arms, sweet and soft as she had been the day she alighted from the coach. Yet there was surprising strength in her. My lips found hers and the banked fires within me glowed and burst into a flame that raced through my body as fire races through a dry forest.

Unsmiling, she drew away from me. "What is the Arapaho marriage ceremony like?"

"There is no real ceremony. A young man's relatives give presents to the girl's brother. If the young man is acceptable, the girl's family then gives presents of equal value to his relatives. A tepee is made and furnished and a feast held. The young man and girl sit together in the tepee, and afterward are considered married."

Dorothy was smiling. She said quickly, "Wait here. Come when I call you."

Puzzled, I watched her climb from the buggy, carrying the buffalo robe that had been over her knees. The sun had dropped behind the cloud bank in the west, and the air was growing cool. Dorothy disappeared into the grove of trees.

After a few moments I heard her call, "Bring the lunch and come on."

I found her sitting on the buffalo robe, which she had spread out on the ground. She had made an odd framework from the branches of trees above it in the shape of a small tepee.

I grinned at her. "What's this?"

Her eyes did not meet mine. Her voice came out small and scared. "It's our tepee, Bill. You have the feast in your hands. The gifts were exchanged long ago, when you saved my life and when I taught you to become a white man."

My understanding came slowly, but when it

did, I was overwhelmed with tenderness for her. I stooped and crawled into the crude, makeshift tepee beside her. My hands trembled as I tore open the lunch.

Barely audible, her voice came to me again. "We can have the white man's marriage ceremony later, can't we, and the Indian ceremony now? I want to be your squaw, Bill. I want to be your squaw tonight, before you go away."

I don't know what was in that lunch. I was filled to bursting with excitement, and with my love for her.

We finished the lunch as dusk turned to darkness in that sharply chill, fragrant grove of cottonwoods. I turned to her, and she came into my arms.

No stars came out above us. Instead, it began to snow, and the soft flakes settled and melted upon the buffalo robe in which we had wrapped ourselves.

Once more I was Sharp Knife. This was my tepee, and this was my squaw. We were no longer two separate people, but one, welded together by darkness, welded by a bond as holy as any ever devised, our desire to belong to each other as long as we both should live.

I returned Dorothy to her home in the dawn hours to find a light burning inside. She was frightened, but she would not let me come in with her. "You must go or you will be in trouble. I'll talk to Father. I'll make him understand."

It seemed cowardly to leave, but I knew that what she said was true. It would be easier on her if I were not present. Besides, the thing was done. She was mine by Indian law, and would soon be mine by the white man's law as well.

I returned the buggy to the stable and got my horse. Mounting, I joined Chivington's army of volunteers as they began to straggle out of town.

They were a ragged bunch, having no regular uniforms, but each dressed as he customarily dressed in civilian life. Most of the officers had uniforms, however, to distinguish them from the men. They rode back and forth along the column, cursing, haranguing the men into some semblance of order.

Southwestward we continued throughout that day and the next, and we camped at the designated rendezvous on Bijou Creek in the afternoon. Now we were in hostile territory, and I spent most of my days scouting the surrounding countryside for signs of the tribes.

Once I crossed the trail of a small hunting party, and followed to the place where they had made their kill, a buffalo cow and calf. Otherwise I found nothing to report to the officers in charge of the expedition.

I hunted and brought in fresh meat for the men, to supplement their scarce rations. Days dragged into weeks, and among the men discontent stirred and increased. "Where the hell is Chivington?" they asked. "What do they think we can do here? Let's get after the goddamn redskins or go on home."

And as though to complicate matters further, a terrific snowstorm struck us. When it cleared, it left two feet of snow piled on the ground. Firewood was scarce and hard to find. The men were not equipped for cold such as this. They suffered as I and my comrades had suffered on our first war party against the white caravans.

November dragged toward its end. But at last, on November 24th, Colonel Chivington rode into our camp with his aides. He was a huge man with a roaring voice and a commanding manner. At once we struck camp and moved out toward the south.

For days we rode our exhausted horses through deep snow, falling too exhausted at night even to remove our wet clothes or dry them out. Dawn would see us moving again.

I scouted incessantly, with orders to bring in every living man I saw. I brought in several, and these were forced to travel along with us, so that no word of our movement could possibly precede us.

I began to feel uneasy in the face of these precautions. What was Chivington planning? Why was it so important that he arrive unannounced?

Was there to be, as I had feared, a sneak attack upon one sleeping village after another?

I scoffed at my doubts, my uneasiness. Chivington had neither the strength for that nor the time. There were six hundred Arapaho near Big Timbers, at least that many Cheyenne at Sand Creek. There was a larger village than both of those combined eastward at Smoky Hill. And Chivington's ninety-day volunteers were due to disband near the end of the mouth.

Covertly I studied Chivington himself, searching for a clue to his intentions somewhere in the character of the man. I failed. He was as unreadable as a page written in a foreign tongue.

We arrived at Fort Lyon, and here Chivington ordered Robert Bent, half-Cheyenne son of William Bent, to join us as a second guide.

I know Chivington was under the impression that Bent obeyed because he was afraid not to obey, but that was not true. I talked to Bent afterward along the route and he told me that his brothers, George and William, and his sister, Julia, were at the Sand Creek camp of Black Kettle. He had acceded to Chivington's order only because he feared the Sand Creek camp to be Chivington's objective.

As indeed it was, though none of us discovered that until it was too late.

Chapter Seventeen

A N AIR OF TENSION hung like a shroud over the bivouac where we rested. The sky began to grow dark with evening, and our fires were a hundred winking eyes against its dull gray background. In the air was the smell of meat roasting on sticks, of coffee, of unwashed men, of horses and manure.

A few hours' rest, for the horses. To hell with the men. Let them sleep when the job was done.

Across the river twenty of our number stood guard over Fort Lyon to see that no one left. I squatted, Indian fashion, beside a small fire and watched its dancing flame moodily. My heart was filled with foreboding that I could not overcome. I told myself it was weariness, the gray, cheerless landscape, the cold, the privation we had endured. I knew it was none of these things. I was afraid—not for myself, but for whatever village Chivington intended to attack.

Jimmy, my single friend among the whites, approached and squatted beside me. Bent came and stood looking silently into the flames at my shoulder. He said, "Jimmy has told me who you are. I have heard of Sharp Knife the Arapaho, friend of Left Hand, son of Red Stone."

I looked up. Bent had spoken in the Arapaho tongue. I said, "I am no longer called Sharp Knife. I am known as William Kelly among the whites." I asked, "What will happen? Do you know?"

Bent shook his head. "Chivington keeps his own counsel. Not even his officers know toward which village we ride. But I suspect it is toward the village of Black Kettle."

"Why?"

He shrugged. "Who can tell what goes on in the mind of the big white chief? But it is known that he fears the Cheyenne more than he fears the Arapaho. Perhaps he intends to attack Black Kettle first and then turn back and attack the Arapaho."

"They should be warned." It was a traitorous utterance that sprang from my lips, but the words were there in my thoughts and I could not push them back.

Bent smiled grimly. He jerked a thumb past his shoulder in a helpless gesture. Behind him lounged half a dozen troopers, who watched him furtively. He said, "My guards. I couldn't leave if I wanted to." He nodded his head toward the opposite side of the fire. "Yours. Chivington trusts you no more than he trusts me."

I said, "How about Jimmy?"

Bent shook his head. "He is sympathetic to the Indians, but he is still a white. And he would never find the village. He does not know the way." He toed a stick into the fire thoughtfully. "No. We have no choice. We must ride along, and do what we can when we can. Perhaps the Cheyenne will not fight. If they do not, they will be safe."

Full dark had fallen as we talked. Bent drifted away, and I watched his guards follow unobtrusively.

Jimmy looked at me, speaking for the first time. "Goddamn it, I wish I hadn't joined up. I don't feel right about this."

"You know what Chivington's plans are?"

"No. I just got a feelin'. Like somethin' dirty and sneaky was up."

I shrugged. "We have no choice but to wait. But I have the same feeling."

Seven-thirty, and suddenly the camp was filled with shouted orders.

Fires were extinguished. In almost complete darkness we found our horses and mounted. Chivington yelled for Bent and me, and we rode to where he sat his horse. He ignored me and looked at Bent. "Ride out. We're headin' fer Black Kettle's outfit on Sand Creek. An' let me warn you, you goddamn breed, no tricks or I'll eat steaks off your goddamn rump for breakfast."

I couldn't see Bent's face, but his body stiffened.

Orders echoed back along the line. We moved

forward at a brisk trot in a column of fours, the men silent, tired, knowing they would be more tired before dawn streaked the sky.

Trot ten minutes, gallop ten. Dismount and lead for ten. Mount and walk, then trot, gallop, dismount, and lead. This way it went all through the night.

Bent tried to lead away a little to the south, but Chivington, guiding himself by the stars, caught the change immediately and returned our heading to the proper one.

Bent led us through a shallow lake, no doubt hoping it would be deep enough to wet our ammunition or bog down the cannon. It was deep enough for neither.

The dawn hours came, and I knew we were close. I dropped back beside Chivington's hulking form. "We're close. Will you want me to ride in and summon Black Kettle and his chiefs?"

"Mebbe. Stay by me and I'll let you know."

Stay by me and I'll let you know! He had no intention of summoning the chiefs. He had no intention of parleying with them. Chivington had known even before he left Denver what he was going to do.

Bent dropped back until he was riding on the other side of Chivington.

Had I but known what Chivington meant to do, I would probably have killed him then, even knowing that I would be killed myself. Bent would have done the same.

But we didn't know.

Gray streaked the eastern sky, outlined the grazing herd of horses that belonged to Black Kettle's village. Whispered orders, and an officer took a detachment and swung away from the column to cut them off from the village.

The rest of the column spread out along a low bluff that commanded a view of the lodges lining the bank of the stream. In painful silence the cannon were wheeled forward and aimed. Men stood by them, ready to fire.

Suddenly below me, in the gradually strengthening light, I saw a cluster of tepees I knew. Left Hand's tepee, and Gray Cloud's, and half a dozen others not so readily distinguishable, but vaguely familiar. They stood a little away from the others, in a circle of their own.

I spoke at once to Chivington. "Left Hand, chief of all the Arapaho, is here." I pointed. "That is his lodge."

Chivington only grunted.

I said, "Left Hand is my friend. Let me go in and talk to him. Let me bring him to you. Whatever you want to accomplish can be done without bloodshed."

He snarled at me, "You stay here, goddamn it!"

I was almost sure then. A hundred times since

have I wished I had acted. But even then it was too late.

A squaw came from one of the Cheyenne tepees with a water skin and headed for the stream. Another came out and looked around at the horizon. A solitary dog barked.

Suddenly the squaw stiffened. She let out a screech and pointed toward the bluff.

The village stirred and came to life. Tepees spewed their occupants as an anthill spews ants when you disturb it with a stick. Voices rose in an uneasy murmur, the awful sound of fear.

From a pole before Black Kettle's tepee an American flag fluttered upward. Beneath it was a pure-white flag, the sign of surrender.

My breath sighed out with infinite relief. Thank God! Thank the God of the Plains Indians for Black Kettle's wisdom.

Black Kettle's voice shouted strongly. "Do not be afraid. We have told the Long Knives at Big Timbers that we wish only peace with the white men, and they have told us to wait, that we are under their protection."

I saw Left Hand come from his tepee and stand before it, arms folded, calmly waiting for the chief of the Long Knives to approach. And I saw—oh, God—I saw the slim form of Singing Wind step from the flap of Gray Cloud's tepee, followed by her brother, Many Elks, and by Gray Cloud himself.

Watching them, I did not see Chivington's arm raise, nor did I see it fall. But I heard the awful bellow of his voice: "Commence firing! This is what you've been yelling for, boys, so make the most of it! I want no prisoners, you understand? Not a goddamn one!"

For an instant I was too stunned to move. Into my dulled mind came Red Stone's words again: "You must choose many times. . . ."

Into my ears, drowning out thoughts, nearly drowning out consciousness, came the shattering boom of a dozen cannon, the following spiteful cracking of half a thousand rifles.

Grapeshot cut through the ranks of the Indians as a scythe cuts through a stand of ripe grain. Bullets whipped through tepees, lashed into the ranks of those still standing.

Worse even than the roar of guns, worse than the panicked screams of the dying, worse than the frightened wail of a lost people was the howl of fiendish glee that rose from the men in our own ranks.

Command was gone. Chivington's bellowing roar was lost, ineffectual. The shouting of his officers went unheeded as the men surged forward, down the side of the bluff.

Now, across the stream, the detachment that had cut off the horses moved in, firing as it went, cutting off the Indians' retreat.

This was a nightmare. I stood rooted for what

seemed an hour. Actually, it could have been no more than a few seconds.

Bent's form became a blur of movement, passing me, running down the slope before me. His voice was raised in an inarticulate scream at the horror of the slaughter. And then I was moving, my eyes on but a single objective, the tepee of Gray Cloud.

Like the wind I ran, straight into the withering hail of fire that came from the men behind.

My white man's clothing saved me. The hail of bullets parted as the men behind me changed their aim to avoid hitting me, and I went on through.

Shock had dulled my mind. This was not real. It couldn't be. In a moment I'd awake, sweating, and find it had all been a dream.

But I did not awake, and it was no dream. I passed a whimpering little girl no older than four, whose chest was a torn mass of blood and flesh. I passed a squaw trying to reach her, crawling with only the use of her hands, for both her shattered legs dragged limply behind.

Tenfold greater than before, my hatred of the whites came back, washing over me like a flood racing down a dry arroyo. My hands tore at my white man's shirt, ripped it from my body. They flung away my hat, so that my black hair streamed out in the wind of my running. At my belt was the Pawnee knife, in my hands the revolving rifle that held the lives of fifteen men in its cylinder.

Left Hand still stood before his tepee, arms folded, refusing to fight the white men. I threw my body at him and we fell in a tangle on the ground. My voice was savage. "Fool! You cannot reason with them. They're drunk from the drinking of Indian blood. Will your death bring peace?"

Left Hand was in as great a state of shock as I was myself. He stared at me uncomprehendingly. I snarled, "Get up and follow me. No one will live who stays here."

Without looking to see whether he followed or not, I scrambled to my feet and ran. My chest heaved with my breathing, working like a giant bellows. It was good to run again, good to depend solely on my own strength.

Ahead of me was the tepee of Gray Cloud. I flung aside its flap, yelling frantically, "Waanibe! Waanibe! Where are you?"

Many Elks sprang at me with a tomahawk. I ducked, caught his body on my back, and flung him bodily through the entrance.

Singing Wind stood in the center of the tepee. Her face was tipped toward the sky, calm with the prayer that had been on her lips. My voice was tense. "Come. Hurry. They have orders to kill each thing that moves. Only in running can there be life today."

Slowly gladness stole into her face. I wanted to see that gladness, wanted to let it wash deliciously over me. But there was no time. Outside the cannon boomed unceasingly, the rifles spat savagely, the Indians died silently or in screaming agony.

I seized her by the wrist and yanked her through the entrance. Left Hand had an unbreakable grip on Many Elks and was saying, "He is one of us. He has always been one of us. And now he has come back to help."

I did not look at them again. Running, dragging the nimble form of Singing Wind behind me, I ran upstream. I stumbled over a body, that of Gray Cloud, felt the resistance of Singing Wind as she tried to pause.

We ran until we were exhausted, and we had much company. Men and women and children ran silently beside us, panting, saving what breath they had for running.

When their breath gave out, they stopped and burrowed ineffectually in the ground, or tried to hide themselves in the grass and brush. The old ones and the very young fell behind first, the younger women next. Pausing in a clump of brush to catch our breath, we watched the advancing whites with hatred and revulsion that was like a sickness.

I saw five squaws hiding beneath a bank of the stream, saw them discovered. Frantically they tore their clothes from their bodies and displayed themselves to prove they were women. The soldiers laughed obscenely and then, as though they were a firing squad and this an execution, they killed every one of the squaws.

Forgetting myself, Singing Wind, and Left Hand too, I raised the revolving rifle. One after another I killed those soldiers until not one remained.

I scooped up a crying baby from a dead squaw's arms and handed it to Singing Wind. I yanked a boy from a clump of brush where he cowered, and dragged him along after me. Two young women joined our group, and we ran until we could run no more. Then we rested again.

And suddenly my shocked mind received yet another shock. I looked at Singing Wind, panting, and asked, "How did Gray Cloud's tepee happen to be among those of the Cheyenne?"

"Back there was all that was left of our village. The white men caught us after you left. Those of us who remained joined Left Hand."

"And what of Beaver Woman? Was she—"

"She was living in the tepee of Left Hand."

I scarcely heard her cry of protest as I sprang to my feet. Before either she or Left Hand or Many Elks could stop me, I was running again, this time toward the village, not away from it.

Singing Wind's voice rose behind me in a lost scream. I glanced behind, saw her struggling in the arms of Many Elks. Then the noise of dying and killing surrounded me, drowning out all other sound.

I knew I would never reach the tepee of Left Hand, doubted if I would find Beaver Woman there even if I did. I knew only my love for Beaver Woman and that I had to know whether she were dead or alive.

I answered a call for help from a squaw in a brush-choked depression, but saw at once she was beyond my help. With her were the bodies of nearly thirty others, all women. She kept repeating over and over, "We sent the little girl out with a white cloth on a stick. They shot her. Then they came here and shot us all. We sent the little girl out with . . ."

I whispered, "Courage, Mother," while my eyes went quickly over the grotesquely sprawled bodies of the dead women with her. Beaver Woman was not among them. I got up and ran on.

Bodies with their bellies ripped open. Bodies with their genitals cut away. A woman cut open, her unborn child lying beside her in a welter of blood. Had white men indeed done this?

And then I found her, mercifully unmutilated. Her face, though wrinkled now, was calm in death, not twisted with agony, as so many of the others were.

I was surprised to discover tears streaming

across my cheeks. I fell to my knees and buried my face in her breasts.

How long I stayed I cannot say. But at last I got to my feet and retraced my steps to the place where I had left the others.

I did not try to avoid death. I did not even notice who or what was around me. I no longer cared.

Left Hand, Many Elks, Singing Wind, and the others were gone. I picked up their trail and followed, and gradually behind me the noise of the carnage faded.

Again the great plain was around me, again its silence was in my ears.

Peace? A mockery. Never again would there be peace between white men and red. Never again while those who could remember Sand Creek lived. Never again while Sharp Knife lived.

Chapter Eighteen

I TRAVELED SLOWLY, for I was very tired. I felt no cold, though I was half naked. I felt no hunger, though I had not eaten in more than twenty-four hours.

I was surprised to discover that it was almost noon. The slaughter had consumed nearly six hours, and it was not done yet.

The trail I followed was plain, for no attempt had been made to hide it. Blood marked it where the crusted snow had cut through bare feet and worn moccasins. Scuffed depressions in the snow marked each place where an exhausted traveler had fallen.

My mind was sick and full of pain. Perhaps no one can see what I had seen this day and wholly retain his sanity. Hate sustained me, hatred and the promise of vengeance I had made.

They wanted war. They should have war. With Left Hand I would unite the tribes of the Great Plains. Comanche, Kiowa, Apache, Arapaho, Cheyenne, Sioux. Together they could put twenty thousand warriors into the field. Add the lesser tribes, Pawnee, Shoshone, Ute, Bannock, Navaho. We would sweep the whites from the plain as a gale sweeps before it a cloud of locusts.

Killing? Mutilation? We would show them our proficiency at both. They had begun it. We would finish it.

In midaftenoon I saw my friends before me, a ragged group, mere specks in the distance. I increased my pace, and half an hour later overtook them.

They had been watching me, and Singing Wind's face shone with joy through the weariness and grime that covered it.

"Did Sharp Knife find his mother?"

I nodded. "Dead."

"I grieve for you." Formal, polite speech. Her eyes spoke her real thoughts, her real compassion, her real love. Many Elks glared at me but said nothing. I knew he was thinking of the way I had left the Arapaho. I knew Singing Wind was thinking that, too.

I said, "Your eyes ask questions but your lips are silent, Waanibe."

"When Sharp Knife is ready, he will speak. It is enough for Waanibe."

I opened my mouth to speak, then snapped it shut. My glance fell away from hers. I was remembering the soft warmth of Dorothy Webb, the shy way she had said, "I want to be your squaw tonight, before you go away." I was remembering the way we had wrapped ourselves in the buffalo robe while the big, soft flakes of snow fell upon our faces and melted there.

I closed my mind and hardened my heart, knowing that I would never see Dorothy again, knowing that even if I stayed with the Arapaho, as I had vowed to do, Singing Wind could not be mine. There would be no time for softness, for love. There was time only for hate, for war, for killing. There was time only for death.

All that afternoon we traveled. Singing Wind carried the baby I had snatched from its dead mother in her arms, wrapped in Many Elks' buckskin shirt. I carried the boy, whose feet were bare and bleeding, part of the time, and Left Hand carried him the rest of the time. Many Elks helped the two exhausted young squaws by turns.

The day put less than ten miles between us and the camp on Sand Creek; less than enough for safety, we knew. Yet somehow none of us seemed to care. If they came, we would exact as high a price as we could for our lives. If they did not come, we would go on.

Night, and the cold was a terrible thing. We had no fire, for we had neither the strength nor the materials with which to make one. And we would have feared the light it would give even if we had had them.

In the lee of a bank undercut by flood we huddled, protecting each other with the warmth of our bodies. The baby cried and coughed, and developed a fever that was hot as flame. The sleeping boy woke screaming with the terror of the day past. Waanibe watched me with eyes that were deep and dark and fathomless.

The young squaws slept, and Many Elks slept. But Left Hand sat staring out into the night's darkness with moody, bitter eyes. "It is my fault, this thing that happened. I trusted the white men. I tried to keep my tribe at peace with them. But I could not control the young men. You know that, Sharp Knife. Their blood runs hot and their minds cannot see the wisdom of patience."

I said harshly, "No longer will we trust the white men. No longer will we live with them at peace. They have begun this war. Now we will bathe the plain with their blood. Their bodies will rot in the sun, and where they have lain the grass will die. But they will take less of our land dead than they take alive."

"You have lived with the whites, Sharp Knife. Are they all liars? Are they all deceitful and treacherous? Are they all cruel?"

I opened my mouth to say that they were. But the words caught in my throat.

Left Hand was smiling sadly. "You do not speak, Sharp Knife. Can it be that you doubt?"

I shook my head. "They are not all treacherous and cruel."

"Perhaps their minds have blinded their eyes. Perhaps they see the Indian not through their eyes, but through their thoughts and prejudices. Our culture is simple and primitive, so they think of us as savages. Our skin is dark, so they believe us inferior. They do not trust us, for our minds follow different paths than theirs. And what they do not trust and understand they seek to destroy. And I think perhaps there is another thing that disturbs them. They know they are stealing our land from us. They are guilty in their minds because they do know this. As long as we are here, they must live with their guilt. So they want to be rid of us."

"You are too generous, Left Hand."

"A man is never too generous with his fellow men."

I felt a stirring of anger. "You are chief of the Arapaho. You are the one who must lead the tribe in war against the whites. You are the one who must help form an alliance of all the tribes of the plains."

He was silent for a long time, but at last he said, "I will never lead my tribe against the whites. When you were but a little boy I told my dream to Red Stone. Have you forgotten it?"

"I have not forgotten." Indeed I had not. Nor had I forgotten my own.

The measured voice of Left Hand and his calm presence had a soothing effect on my confused mind. And for the first time I began to doubt the wisdom of my vow.

Ha-sananen had told Left Hand, "The white men are as many as the grains of sand in the river bed. You must learn to live at peace with them."

I asked, no longer sure of myself, "What must I do, Left Hand? Tell me what I must do."

"I cannot tell you, Sharp Knife. Only your own heart can tell you that. Each man must follow the star he has chosen to follow, wherever it leads. Perhaps my star leads to destruction. But I have chosen it and will follow it until I die." He subsided into silence that was almost trancelike.

I thought of the things that had been between William Kelly and Dorothy Webb—the long days of study, of never ending patience and understanding on her part. I thought of the gift she had given the night before I'd left—the gift of herself.

My blood stirred and warmed at the thought of her, soft, womanly, but with a tenacious strength for all of that.

Feeling the eyes of Singing Wind upon me, I turned my glance to her. Like a stricken doe she watched me, as though she waited for the death blow of my words.

Much lay between Singing Wind and Sharp Knife. A childhood of carefree play, a lifetime of loyalty. A love that had budded but never blossomed, but which could blossom gloriously if I but said the word.

Blossom gloriously? Was I mad? I could never take Singing Wind as my wife. I would be on the warpath with the rest of the tribe. For in spite of Left Hand's standing as chief of the Arapaho, there would be no peace. The smaller chiefs would override his edicts; the "dog soldiers" would refuse to enforce them. He would become a chief with no standing, no authority.

Dawn came, and my mind was still confused. Again we staggered along through the blinding waste of snow toward the friendly camp at Smoky Hill. And again we covered less than ten miles.

During the day the baby died, and because we had no strength or implements with which to dig in the frozen ground, we left his body in the crotch of a tree, beyond the reach of wolves. And that day one of the young squaws fell exhausted from cold and begged us to go on without her. We carried her between us, but it was no use. Before sunset, she too died.

Again that night we huddled in the lee of a bank, waiting out the bitter cold. And again that night Left Hand and I talked.

Both of us were lightheaded with hunger and weariness. It was almost as it had been so long ago when I fasted on the mountaintop, waiting for Ha-sananen to speak.

And because of this I welcomed weakness and hunger and weariness. Perhaps God would come to me again. Perhaps He would calm my tortured mind with His words of wisdom. Perhaps He would show me which star to follow, bright white star, or red star of the Arapaho.

Left Hand said, "Among the Arapaho you will be but another warrior. We have many warriors, though none more brave than Sharp Knife."

"What are you trying to say?"

He appeared not to have heard, but went on in the same tone. "There is much bitterness among the Arapaho and Cheyenne. If Sharp Knife found their distrust difficult before, he will find it doubly so now."

I waited, for now I could see that Left Hand was not consciously talking to me, but was merely thinking aloud. "Among the Arapaho, Sharp Knife will be but another rifle. Yet among the whites, he could be a great friend to his people."

"You mean as a spy?"

He swung his head fiercely. "I do *not* mean as a spy. I mean as a teacher. Sharp Knife could teach the whites to understand us better. He could teach them that we are not prairie animals, but people who feel and think as they do. People who cry when they are hurt, who laugh when they are happy, who bleed when they are wounded, and who die no more willingly than they. Sharp Knife has learned to read the words in the white man's books. He has learned to write their words so that others may read."

Singing Wind sat beside me as though frozen. Her breathing was barely audible.

Left Hand said, "Sharp Knife could write the story of the Arapaho so that the white men could read it. Who knows what good the writing might do? Perhaps if they understood us, they would not hate us. Perhaps then they would see that beneath our clothes and our customs we are just as they themselves are."

A long sigh escaped the lips of Singing Wind. I took her hand in mine, and it was very cold. I asked, "Would you have me stay?"

Her voice was small. "Sharp Knife must follow his star. Left Hand has shown him that star, and it is not red, but white. Singing Wind will remember Sharp Knife. She will tell her children of his bravery and his kindness as proof that there is indeed much good among the whites."

My throat closed, and for a moment I clung to her hand as a drowning man clings to the branch of a floating log. Then I released it and my mind was again remembering Dorothy, my wife by Indian law, soon to be my wife by the white man's law as well.

The years ahead would not be easy. But always she would be with me, giving me strength and purpose, giving freely of herself as she always had.

We would reach Smoky Hill. I was sure of that now. My Indian brothers would give me clothes and weapons and a horse. They would feed me and let me rest.

Hating the race to which I belonged, they

would yet raise their hands in farewell as I rode away. For I was Sharp Knife the Arapaho, and as Sharp Knife I would be their champion among the whites.

| Books are produced in the United States using U.S.-based materials | Books are printed using a revolutionary new process called THINKtech™ that lowers energy usage by 70% and increases overall quality | Books are durable and flexible because of Smyth-sewing | Paper is sourced using environmentally responsible foresting methods and the paper is acid-free |

Center Point Large Print

600 Brooks Road / PO Box 1
Thorndike, ME 04986-0001 USA

(207) 568-3717

US & Canada:
1 800 929-9108
www.centerpointlargeprint.com